Klipp & Klar Lerntrainer

Herausgegeben von Walter Kowalczyk und Klaus Ottich

Dr. Walter Kowalczyk, Jahrgang 1949, ist Schulpsychologe und als Lehrbeauftragter an der Universität Hannover tätig. Er ist Mitglied in der Aktion Humane Schule und in der Deutschen Gesellschaft für Lesen und Schreiben (DGLS).
Klaus Ottich, Jahrgang 1942, ist Oberstudienrat und arbeitet als Lehrer für Deutsch und Geschichte an einem Gymnasium.
Beide Herausgeber sind in der regionalen und überregionalen Fortbildung tätig. Sie haben zahlreiche Bücher und Aufsätze zu den Themen «Zusammenarbeit zwischen Elternhaus und Schule» und «Lernförderung» veröffentlicht und sich intensiv mit der Lern- und Gedächtnisforschung befasst. Im Rowohlt Taschenbuch Verlag sind bereits von ihnen erschienen: «Der Elternabend» (Nr. 19182), «Schülern auf die Sprünge helfen» (Nr. 19775) und «Erfolgreich in der Schule» (Nr. 60189).

Beate Günther, Jahrgang 1962, ist Lehrerin für Englisch und Französisch an einem Gymnasium und Referentin in der Regionalen Lehrerfortbildung.
Peter Perrey, Jahrgang 1940, ist Lehrer für Englisch und Deutsch, Fachvorstand Englisch und Leiter des Amerika-Austausches an einem Gymnasium. Er war vorher u. a. Lehrer für Deutsch und Englisch an einer amerikanischen Schule und Lehrbeauftragter der University of Maryland.

Beate Günther / Peter Perrey

Englisch, 8. und 9. Klasse

Grammatik: Artikel, ‘progressive form’, Relativsatz, Passiv

Mit Vokabeltrainer

rororo
Rowohlt

Die Schreibweise entspricht den Regeln
der neuen Rechtschreibung.

Originalausgabe
Lektorat Katrin Helmstedt

Veröffentlicht im Rowohlt Taschenbuch
Verlag GmbH, Reinbek bei Hamburg, August 1998

Umschlaggestaltung Susanne Müller
Illustrationen Christof Tisch
Reihentypografie Iris Farnschläder
Layout Christina Modi
Gedruckt auf Arctic Volume 115 g/qm
der Håfreströms AB Schweden
Gesetzt aus der Minion und Trade Gothic
auf Apple Macintosh in QuarkXPress 3.32
Gesamtherstellung Clausen & Bosse, Leck
Printed in Germany
ISBN 3 499 60395 0

Inhalt

Liebe Eltern,

können Sie inzwischen das Frühlingsgedicht genauso gut aufsagen wie Ihr Kind? Fühlen Sie sich in Ihre eigene Schulzeit zurückversetzt, weil Sie wieder über der Bruchrechnung brüten? Oder versuchen Sie, einen englischen Text zu entschlüsseln, obwohl Sie die Sprache selbst kaum beherrschen? Möglicherweise sind Sie in heller Aufregung, denn Ihr Kind hat schon wieder eine «Klassenarbeit verhauen». Vielleicht ist sogar die «Versetzung gefährdet»?

Wie viele Nachmittage haben Sie schon mit Ihrem Kind für die Schule gepaukt, sich Aufgaben ausgedacht, nach Erklärungen gesucht und sich überlegt, ob Lösungswege richtig oder falsch sind? Aber nicht nur das zerrt an Ihren Nerven, auch die Stimmung ist mies. Wenn Sie mit Ihrem Kind gemeinsam für die Schule büffeln, ist dies sicher oft mit Auseinandersetzungen und Tränen verbunden. «Ich kapier das eh nie.» – «Ich will endlich zu meinen Freunden.» – «Mein Lehrer hat mir das aber ganz anders erklärt.» Und Sie hatten sich den Nachmittag wahrscheinlich auch schöner vorgestellt.

Selbst wenn Sie im Moment gestresst und ratlos sind: In der Regel können Kinder jeden Lernstoff begreifen. Wichtig ist, dass durch eine abwechslungsreiche Darbietung des Stoffes individuelles Lernen ermöglicht und Freude an der Auseinandersetzung mit einem Thema gefördert wird. Hier liegt eine Stärke der *klipp & klar Lerntrainer.* Ein weiterer Vorteil ist, dass Ihr Kind mit den *klipp & klar Lerntrainern* **selbständig** arbeiten kann: Der Lernstoff wird verständlich, anschaulich und in kleinen Schritten dargestellt. Lerntipps erleichtern Ihrem Kind das Verstehen, Anwenden und Behalten. Durch Tests wird geprüft, ob das Gelernte auch sicher sitzt. An einigen Stellen ist es sinnvoll, dass Sie Ihre Hilfe anbieten. Dort finden Sie dieses Zeichen (siehe rechts), z. B. bei der Terminplanung für die Wiederholungen.

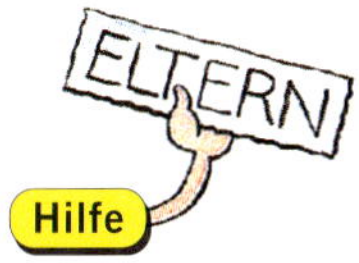

Mit den *klipp & klar Lerntrainern* können nicht nur erfolgreich Probleme in bestimmten Fächern ausgeräumt werden, sie eignen sich auch hervorragend, wenn Ihr Kind sein Wissen bei einzelnen Themen aufpolieren oder sich gezielt auf eine Klassenarbeit vorbereiten möchte. Die *klipp & klar Lerntrainer* helfen Ihnen dabei, dass die Nachmittage mit Ihrem Kind wieder entspannter verlaufen.

Walter Kowalczyk und Klaus Ottich

Liebe Lehrerin, lieber Lehrer,

in jeder Klasse begegnen Sie Schülerinnen und Schülern, die Probleme mit bestimmten Themen haben. Besorgte Eltern haben sich an Sie gewandt und um Rat und spezielle Lerntipps gebeten. Viele sind unsicher, wie sie ihr Kind erfolgreich unterstützen können, und fühlen sich beim Erklären schulischer Lerninhalte verständlicherweise überfordert. Das gemeinsame Üben belastet häufig die ganze Familie. Sicher gibt es auch Schülerinnen und Schüler, denen Sie gern geeignetes Übungsmaterial empfehlen würden, damit sie selbständig Schwächen abbauen und ihre Leistungen verbessern können.

Überzeugen Sie sich selbst: Mit den *klipp & klar Lerntrainern* kann jeder Schüler seine Defizite selbständig aufarbeiten:

- Der Lernstoff wird verständlich, anschaulich und in kleinen Schritten dargestellt.
- Die abwechslungsreiche Darbietung des Stoffes fördert individuelles Lernen und die Motivation, sich mit einem Thema auseinander zu setzen.
- Alle Fachbegriffe werden erläutert, sodass Verständnisprobleme gar nicht erst entstehen.
- Lerntipps erleichtern das Verstehen, Anwenden und Behalten.
- Das Üben in sinnvollen Lernetappen unterstützt den Lernerfolg.
- Wiederholungsübungen sichern langfristig den Lernfortschritt.
- Durch Tests wird überprüft, ob das Gelernte auch sitzt.

Und auch Sie selbst können die *klipp & klar Lerntrainer* mit Gewinn nutzen:

- als Vorbereitung für Ihren Unterricht,
- als Differenzierungsmaterial für Ihre Klasse,
- als Lernprogramm für Ihren Förderunterricht.

Wir wünschen Ihnen viel Erfolg für Ihre Arbeit!
Walter Kowalczyk und Klaus Ottich

Liebe Schülerin, lieber Schüler,
so kannst du mit diesem Buch arbeiten:

1. Bevor du anfängst, blättere einfach mal in diesem Buch: Wo geht es um den Relativsatz? Hast du die Wiederholungsaufgaben und den Lösungsteil entdeckt? Wo findest du das Lesezeichen? Vielleicht fallen dir einige Seiten auf, die dich neugierig machen.
2. Wähle dir ein Thema aus oder beginne gleich auf der nächsten Seite.
3. Lies dir die Erklärungen genau durch. Wiederhole sie mit eigenen Worten. So erkennst du, ob du sie wirklich verstanden hast.
4. Arbeite jeden Tag 20 Minuten lang mit diesem Buch. Schreibe mit einem Bleistift, damit du Fehler leichter verbessern kannst. Radiere falsche Lösungen aus und bearbeite diese Aufgaben noch einmal.
5. Wichtig! Kontrolliere und berichtige deine Lösungen sofort. Hier ist es sicher hilfreich, wenn deine Eltern, Geschwister oder Mitschüler dich dabei unterstützen. Danach: Schluss für heute.

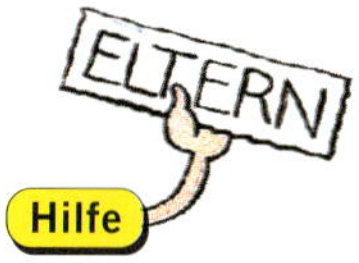

6. Wenn du am nächsten Tag weiterarbeitest, lies zunächst noch einmal die Erklärungen des letzten Abschnitts durch. Dann weißt du wieder, worum es geht.
7. Die Wiederholungsübungen (ab Seite 59) helfen dir, den Lernstoff länger zu behalten.
8. Am Schluss des Buches findest du Tests zu den einzelnen Kapiteln. Trage dein persönliches Testergebnis in das Bewertungsschema ein und ermittle deine Note. Es handelt sich bei den Tests nicht um vollständige Klassenarbeiten, sondern um den grammatischen Teil, der in der Regel ein Drittel der Arbeit ausmacht.

Wenn du in Schwierigkeiten gerätst, bitte deine Eltern, Freunde, Geschwister, Mitschüler oder Lehrer, dir zu helfen. Viel Erfolg und Spaß bei der Arbeit mit diesem Buch!

Der Artikel

Im Englischen gibt es nur einen **bestimmten** und einen **unbestimmten Artikel** (*definite article* und *indefinite article*).
Der **bestimmte Artikel** heißt 'the'.
Der **unbestimmte Artikel** heißt 'a' (vor Vokalanlaut 'an').

Hilfe

Zum Vokalanlaut lies kurz auf Seite 18 nach.

Der bestimmte Artikel ('definite article')

Der **bestimmte Artikel** *(definite article)* heißt so, weil er sich auf eine bestimmte Person oder eine bestimmte Sache bezieht.

Anwendung

Der **bestimmte Artikel** 'the' wird benutzt, wenn es sich um einen **konkreten Einzelfall** handelt.

Beispiel

The life of **President Lincoln** has often been filmed.

Tipp

Den Einzelfall erkennst du daran, dass eine nähere Bestimmung im Satz vorkommt, z. B.
- eine Ergänzung mit 'of'
- ein Relativsatz
- ein Adjektiv.

Beispiel

the life of President Lincoln (Ergänzung mit 'of')
the water which you see (Relativsatz)
the beautiful lady (Adjektiv)

Sprichst du von Personen, Sachen oder Vorgängen im allgemeinen Sinne, darfst du 'the' nicht benutzen. Für uns Deutsche ist das eine häufige Fehlerquelle, denn im Deutschen benutzen wir in solchen Fällen einen Artikel.

Achtung, Stolperstein!

Beispiel

Life is difficult. Das Leben ist schwierig.

Werden Abstrakta nicht näher bestimmt, so stehen sie immer **ohne** 'the'.

Beispiel

I love nature. Ich liebe die Natur.

Hinweis

Häufig gebrauchte Abstrakta sind z. B.:
'life', 'death', 'history', 'art', 'nature', 'joy', 'fear', 'fun'.

Übung 1 Mit oder ohne 'the'?
With or without 'the'?

Poor grandma!

1. Grandma, "__________ society we are living in is no longer __________ society which existed when I was a girl."
2. Alice, "Well, __________ society has to change, just as __________ life changes all __________ time."
3. Grandma, "Just think of __________ buses which we have to use these days. Wherever you go __________ buses are always late."
4. Alice, "That's not true. __________ bus which I took was punctual."
5. Grandma, "Taxis are so expensive, __________ water we drink is polluted, __________ meat we eat is contaminated."
6. Alice, "Oh stop it, grandma. I still like to drink __________ water and to eat __________ meat."
7. Grandma, "But __________ most people don't eat __________ meat any longer."
8. Alice, "Most of __________ young people I know don't panic that much. Of course, you are right. One has to be careful and pay attention to what happens. But __________ panicking doesn't help."

Überprüfe die Übung mit Hilfe des Lösungsteils.

Den bestimmten Artikel 'the' gebrauchst du immer dann, wenn du von einem **Gebäude als Ort** sprichst, nicht aber vom Zweck (von der Funktion), den dieses Gebäude erfüllt.

Beispiel

We'll meet at **the** school.
Last Sunday we went to **the** church to listen to the Bach concert.

In beiden Beispielen wird nur gesagt, wo etwas stattfinden soll bzw. schon stattgefunden hat.

Wenn aber der Zweck eines Gebäudes oder einer Einrichtung gemeint ist, musst du 'the' **weglassen.**

Beispiel

We'll go to school at about 8 o'clock.
Every Sunday we go to church.
The murderer had to go to prison.
Mum has to go to hospital for two weeks.

In diesen Beispielen geht es jeweils um den Zweck der Gebäude. Wir gehen zur Schule, um dort zu lernen. Wir gehen zur Kirche, um am Gottesdienst teilzunehmen. Der Mörder musste ins Gefängnis, um eine Haftstrafe zu verbüßen, und Mum muss ins Krankenhaus, um behandelt zu werden.

Übung 2 Füge, wo nötig, den bestimmten Artikel ein.
Insert the definite article where necessary.

1. Well, to get to Louise's house, go to __________ church and then turn right.
2. When we were in Paris, I took a lot of photos of Notre Dame. We also went to __________ church there.
3. When did you leave __________ school?
   I left __________ school in 1992 and then I went to __________ university.
4. Grandma had to go to __________ hospital to be operated on. I often go to __________ hospital to see her.
5. Let's meet at __________ cinema. Then we can go to __________ church to listen to the Mozart concert.
6. I have to be home early because I have to wake up my son who has to go to __________ school at 8 o'clock.

Überprüfe die Übung mit Hilfe des Lösungsteils.

Vor allen **Namen für Musikinstrumente** steht der **bestimmte Artikel**.

Beispiel John plays the piano and Eileen plays the flute.

Bekannte Gebäude, Denkmäler, Sehenswürdigkeiten, Straßen und Plätze stehen manchmal mit und manchmal ohne den **bestimmten Artikel** 'the'.

Lerne die folgenden Bezeichnungen wie Vokabeln auswendig.

mit 'the'	ohne 'the'
the Tower	Buckingham Palace
the Houses of Parliament	Westminster Abbey
the Mall	Big Ben
the White House	St. Paul's Cathedral
the Statue of Liberty	Downing Street
the British Museum	Fifth Avenue
the World Trade Center	Nelson's Column
the Strand	Whitehall
the Globe	Trafalgar Square
the Chamber of Horrors	Fleet Street
the Thames Flood Barrier	Brooklyn Bridge
the Empire State Building	Broadway
the UN Building	Central Park

Hinweis

Hier einige Beispiele, die häufig vorkommen.

Hast du dir schon das Kapitel «Der Vokabeltrainer» (Seite 79–84) durchgelesen? Dort erhältst du Tipps, die es dir erleichtern, Vokabeln zu lernen und zu behalten.
Lege für die oben aufgelisteten Beispiele eine besondere Seite in deinem Vokabeltrainer an (vergleiche Seite 79–80).

Tipp

Lerne auch die folgenden Wendungen wie Vokabeln auswendig.

all the (time)	–	die ganze (Zeit)
half the (price)	–	den halben (Preis)
most of the (dogs)	–	die meisten der (Hunde)

most (children) – die meisten (Kinder)

Achtung, Stolperstein!

Übung 3 Entscheide, ob du den bestimmten Artikel benutzen musst oder nicht.

Decide whether or not to use the definite article.

David und Nick treffen sich erstmalig. Ihr Musiklehrer hat das Treffen arrangiert.

1. David, "Hi, Nick. I'm David. Mr. Burton told me that we would play __________ piano together."
2. Nick, "Hi, David. Sorry, I'm not playing __________ piano, I'm playing __________ violin."
3. David, "Oh, probably Mr. Burton thought that __________ piano and __________ violin would sound good together."
4. Nick, "Probably. When do you think can we practise?" David, "On Mondays. I've all __________ afternoon to practise with you."
5. Nick, "That is fine for the Easter holidays, however, usually I haven't got all __________ Monday afternoons for myself. But what about Saturdays?"
6. David, "That's fine. All __________ Saturdays are free. Except in the Easter holidays, we will go to London."
7. Nick, "Oh, then you must go to __________ Hyde Park to go skating."
8. David, "My parents want me to see __________ Buckingham Palace, __________ Tower, __________ Thames Flood Barrier, __________ Houses of Parliament, __________ St. Paul's Cathedral, etc."
9. Nick, "Oh, poor you."

Überprüfe die Übung mit Hilfe des Lösungsteils.

Lernposter: Der bestimmte Artikel ('definite article')

the

Mit 'the', wenn es sich um eine näher bestimmte Aussage handelt.
The life of President Lincoln was extra-ordinary.

Musikinstrumente
John plays **the** fiddle.

Gebäude, wenn der **Ort** gemeint ist.
Let's meet in front of **the** church.

Einige bekannte Gebäude, Denkmäler, Straßen, Plätze
z. B. **the** Tower (of London), **the** Houses of Parliament

all **the**, half **the**, most of **the**

ohne 'the'

Ohne 'the', wenn es sich um eine allgemein gültige Aussage handelt.
Life is difficult.

Einige bekannte Gebäude, Denkmäler, Straßen, Plätze
z. B. Buckingham Palace, Westminster Abbey

Gebäude, wenn der **Zweck** gemeint ist.
On Sunday we go to church.

some, much, more, most

Kopiere und vergrößere dir die Übersicht auf DIN-A3-Format und hänge sie über deinen Schreibtisch an die Wand.

Der unbestimmte Artikel ('indefinite article')

Der **unbestimmte Artikel** hat zwei Formen: 'a' und 'an'.

Hinweis
Vokallaute sind a, e, i, o, u.

Aus 'a' wird 'an', wenn das Wort, das folgt, mit einem Vokal**laut** beginnt.
Es heißt also: 'an orange', weil das Nomen 'orange' mit dem Vokal [ɒ] anlautet.
Es heißt auch: 'an hour', weil das Nomen 'hour' mit dem Vokal [aʊ] anlautet.
Es kommt also nicht auf den ersten Buchstaben des folgenden Wortes an, sondern auf dessen **Anlaut**.

Achtung, Stolperstein!

So heißt es z. B. bei dem Nomen 'unit': 'a unit', denn das Nomen 'unit' fängt, wenn man es spricht, nicht mit einem Vokallaut an, sondern mit dem Konsonanten [j].

Tipp

Sprich dir im Zweifelsfall die Wörter vor. Dann hörst du, ob sie mit einem Vokal oder einem Konsonanten anlauten.
Dies gilt auch für einzelne Buchstaben, z. B. bei der Abkürzung MP [em pi:]. MP = Member of Parliament.

Übung 4

Setze 'a' oder 'an' ein. a, e, i, o, u
Fill in 'a' or 'an'.

1. a car
2. a doctor
3. an apple
4. an eye
5. an underground station
6. a uniform
7. a home
8. an hour
9. an ice-cream
10. a helicopter
11. an order
12. an uncle
13. an elephant
14. an orange

Überprüfe die Übung mit Hilfe des Lösungsteils.

Diese Regel gilt nicht nur für die Nomen, sondern auch für Adjektive, die auf den **unbestimmten Artikel** folgen.

Die Form des **unbestimmten Artikels** kann sich ändern, wenn ein anderes Adjektiv gewählt wird oder das Adjektiv wegfällt.

Beispiel

a new computer	an ant
an expensive computer	a big ant

Übung 5

Setze 'a' oder 'an' ein.
Fill in 'a' or 'an'.

1. ___an___ extra job
2. ___a___ useful exercise
3. ___an___ interesting job
4. ___a___ fantastic chance
5. ___a___ magic hour
6. ___an___ obvious mistake
7. ___an___ interesting woman
8. ___an___ honest man
9. ___an___ even number
10. ___a___ surprising example
11. ___a___ comfortable chair
12. ___an___ angry child
13. ___an___ understandable question
14. ___a___ good pupil
15. ___an___ excellent student

Überprüfe die Übung mit Hilfe des Lösungsteils.

Anwendung

Der **unbestimmte Artikel** ('a' oder 'an') steht vor **Berufsbezeichnungen** und vor einem **Titel im Singular**.

Beispiel

My dad is **a** policeman.
Mr Davis is **an** MP. [em pi:]
Mrs Black is **a** doctor.

Aber:
Mr Stewart and Mrs Green are busdrivers.

Entscheide, ob der unbestimmte Artikel ('a' oder 'an') gebraucht wird oder nicht.
Decide whether or not to use the indefinite article.

Übung 6

Talking about children

1. Mrs Barton, "Sue has always wanted to become ________ doctor. But now she wants to become ________ farmer. I can't understand that. My husband is ________ judge and I'm ________ dentist. We don't have ________ farmers in our family. If she really wants to become ________ farmer she will need a farm – we don't have one and we don't have the money to buy one either."
2. Mrs Dent, "Don't worry. When my son was Sue's age he wanted to be ________ ambulance driver because he loved the idea of driving cars. Today he is ________ reporter. Don't you remember what you wanted to be when you were young?"
3. Mrs Barton, "Yes, I wanted to be ________ ice-skater!"
4. Mrs Dent, "And what ________ wonderful dentist you are now!"

Überprüfe die Übung mit Hilfe des Lösungsteils.

Der **unbestimmte Artikel** ('a' oder 'an') steht auch vor Wörtern, die eine **Gruppenzugehörigkeit** bezeichnen. Die Gruppe kann z. B. eine Nation, eine Partei oder eine Religionsgemeinschaft sein.

Beispiel

Mr McCourt is a Scotsman. John is a Socialist.
Mrs Watson is a Protestant.

Du kennst aus dem Deutschen das Wort «pro». Dies kannst du entweder mit dem **unbestimmten Artikel** 'a' oder 'an' oder aber mit dem Wort 'per' übersetzen.

Beispiel

In the holidays we walked 16 miles a day.
Oder: In the holidays we walked 16 miles per day.

Butter costs £ 3 a kilo.
Oder: Butter costs £ 3 per kilo.

Der **unbestimmte Artikel** 'a' oder 'an' steht auch vor bestimmten Wendungen. Lerne sie auswendig.

quite a nice day	– ein ziemlich netter Tag
rather a good friend	– ein ziemlich guter Freund
(hier auch: a rather good friend)	
such a friendly boy	– so ein netter Junge
what a superb meal	– was für ein vorzügliches Essen
half a page	– eine halbe Seite
once a day	– einmal am Tag
as a boy	– als Junge

Tipp

Die Vokabeln 'quite' und 'rather' heißen beide «ziemlich».

Hinweis

«Als» + Nomen ist nicht zu verwechseln mit «als» zu Beginn eines Nebensatzes (Konjunktion):
als Junge – 'as a boy'
als ich ein Junge war – 'when I was a boy'

Entscheide, ob du 'a' oder 'an' benutzen musst oder nicht.
Decide whether or not you have to use 'a' or 'an'.

Übung 7

1. Dear Grandma,

   Yesterday I received your letter. What ________ surprise when I opened it and found ________ cheque for £ 50.

2. As you know, I usually get my pocket money once ________ month most of the time.

3. I don't have any more money after two weeks. It is fantastic to have ________ grandma who understands that.

4. What ________ problem money had been for me before your generous cheque arrived.

5. You know ________ life is very expensive. Even as ________ teenager you always have problems with money.

6. Coke costs 80 p ________ glass, coffee 50 p ________ cup at school. Jeans cost about £ 40 ________ pair.

7. You write that you remember very well what ________ life was like when you were young. Did you have problems with money as ________ young girl as well? Yes, really.

8. Mum never understands me. She thinks that I'm spending too much money anyway. Was Mum like that when she was ________ young girl?

   Much love and thank you so much!

   Yours,

   Susan

Überprüfe die Übung mit Hilfe des Lösungsteils.

Lernposter:

Der unbestimmte Artikel ('indefinite article')

'a' oder 'an'

Berufsbezeichnungen
My dad is a policeman.
My dad is an architect.

Gruppenzugehörigkeit
Mr McCourt is a Scotsman.
Mr Antonelli is an Italian.

Als Übersetzung von «pro»
In the last holidays we walked 2 miles an hour and 16 miles a day.

In bestimmten Wendungen
quite a nice day
an interesting day
rather a good friend
rather an old friend

Kopiere und vergrößere dir die Übersicht auf DIN-A3-Format und hänge sie über deinen Schreibtisch an die Wand.

Die ‘progressive form’

Anwendung

Die **progressive form** (Verlaufsform) verwendest du, wenn du einen Vorgang von **begrenzter Dauer** darstellen willst. Er wird zu einem **bestimmten Zeitpunkt** betrachtet. Du denkst dabei an den Verlauf der Handlung, die **noch nicht beendet** ist. Der Vorgang kann in der Gegenwart, in der Vergangenheit oder auch in der Zukunft ablaufen. Deshalb kannst du die **progressive form** auch in allen grammatischen Zeiten bilden.

Tipp

Die ‘progressive form’ wird auch ‘continuous form’ genannt.

Beispiel

Vorgang von begrenzter Dauer, der noch nicht beendet ist → „I am watching TV“

1. Right now, I **am watching** TV.

„Right now“ → **bestimmter Zeitpunkt**; „am watching“ → **progressive form**

Vorgang von begrenzter Dauer, der noch nicht beendet ist → „because it is getting dark“

2. It must be late because it **is getting** dark.

„It must be late“ → **bestimmter Zeitpunkt**; „is getting“ → **progressive form**

Vorgang von begrenzter Dauer, der noch nicht beendet war → „Eileen was doing her homework“

3. Eileen **was doing** her homework when I called.

„was doing“ → **progressive form**; „when I called“ → **bestimmter Zeitpunkt**

Die Grundregeln werden in den drei Beispielen deutlich:
Es handelt sich in allen Fällen um **noch nicht abgeschlossene Vorgänge** von **begrenzter Dauer**.

In Satz 1 ist die Rede davon, dass ich gerade dabei sei fernzusehen – das werde ich nicht endlos fortsetzen.
In Satz 2 heißt es, dass es gerade dunkel werde – es ist also bald der Punkt erreicht, an dem es ganz dunkel sein wird.
In Satz 3 wird berichtet, dass Eileen gerade Hausaufgaben gemacht habe – auch diese Tätigkeit hat erfahrungsgemäß bald ein Ende.

In allen drei Beispielen werden die Vorgänge auch **zu bestimmten Zeiten** betrachtet:

In Satz 1 ist der Zeitpunkt 'right now', also gerade jetzt. Die zu wählende Form ist deshalb das *present progressive.*
In Satz 2 ist es abends ('it must be late'). Das *present progressive* wird hier gewählt, weil der Sprecher etwas über einen gerade ablaufenden Vorgang aussagt.
In Satz 3 ist der bestimmte Zeitpunkt 'when I called' (als ich anrief). Da der Zeitpunkt in der Vergangenheit liegt, ist hier das *past progressive* anzuwenden.

Die Verben 'watch' und 'do' bezeichnen einen Tätigkeitsablauf, das Verb 'get' gibt eine Veränderung wieder.

Die **progressive form** kann nur von solchen Verben gebildet werden, die einen **Tätigkeitsablauf** oder eine **Veränderung** ausdrücken. Man nennt solche Verben «dynamische Verben» *(dynamic verbs).*

Beispiel

Die Verben 'change', 'run', 'throw', 'work', 'write' sind weitere *dynamic verbs.*

Verben, die einen Zustand, eine Eigenschaft oder eine Beziehung bezeichnen, heißen «statische Verben» *(state verbs).*

Tipp

Beispiel

Die Verben 'hate', 'like', 'know', 'want', 'wish' sind *state verbs.*

Die **progressive form** ist keine selbständige grammatische Zeit, sondern eine Betrachtungs- oder Sichtweise, unter der du eine Handlung darstellst.
Im Deutschen gibt es nur zwei Fügungen, in denen du Ähnliches wie die **progressive form** benutzt. Deshalb ist diese Form für dich ungewohnt.

Diese beiden Fügungen gibt es im Deutschen:
– «beim» + nominalisiertes Verb

Beispiel

beim Schreiben sein
Sie ist wieder beim Schreiben. She **is writing** again.

– «am» + nominalisiertes Verb

Beispiel

am Husten sein
Sie ist dauernd am Husten. She **is** constantly **coughing.**

Üblicherweise gibt man die **progressive form** im Deutschen jedoch mit Hilfe des Wortes «gerade» wieder.

Beispiel

He **is writing** a letter. Er schreibt gerade einen Brief.

Die **progressive form** steht im Gegensatz zur *simple form* (einfache Form, Normalform). Die *simple form* bezeichnet
- eine abgeschlossene Handlung,
- das Ergebnis einer Handlung oder
- etwas, das immer wieder geschieht, sowie
- Tatsachen.

Im Deutschen benutzen wir in der Regel die Normalform.

Beispiel

1. We **visited** the Hard Rock Café yesterday.
2. Germany **wins** the soccer cup.
3. Bob **rides** his bike to school. (D. h., er fährt gewöhnlich nicht mit dem Schulbus.)
4. Vinegar **smells** sour.

Tipp

Die Vokabel 'vinegar' heißt Essig.

Hinweis

Neben der **progressive form** und der *simple form* gibt es noch die *emphatic form* (Betonungsform). Sie wird im klipp & klar Lerntrainer Englisch 9. und 10. Klasse (rororo 60527) behandelt.

Bildung

So bildest du die **progressive form**:

Form von 'be' + *present participle* des Vollverbs
(Vollverb + 'ing')

Die grammatische Zeit der **progressive form** bestimmt sich nach der grammatischen Zeit, in der die Form von 'be' steht.

Beispiel

present tense	She **is** listening to music right now.
present perfect	She **has been** listening to music for two hours already. It is about time to stop.
past tense	She **was** listening to music when her brother came in.
past perfect	She **had been** listening to music for a while when her father told her to turn down the volume.
future I	She **will be** listening to music for some time tomorrow afternoon.
future II	She **will have been** listening to music for hours at this time tomorrow.
conditional I	She **would be** listening to music she said.
conditional II	She **would have been** listening to music if she had had the time.

Hinweis

Das *conditional I* und das *conditional II* der **progressive form** werden – statt mit 'would' (würde) – auch häufig mit 'could' (könnte) oder mit 'should' (sollte) gebildet.

Beispiel

Let's take an umbrella along. It **could be** raining when we arrive.
We **should have been** working instead of playing football.

Übung 8 Setze die Verben in die *progressive form* der angegebenen Zeiten.
Put the verbs into the progressive form of the given tenses.

Hilfe

Zu den Zeiten lies noch einmal die Seite 29.

1. Jerry came into the counselor's office when Mr Ken Reeves, the counselor, (talk, *past tense*) ______________________ ________________ on the phone.
2. Mr Reeves said, "Jerry, I (talk, *present tense*) __________ ___________________ to a parent right now. Could you wait outside, please?"
3. Jerry (sit, *past perfect*) ______________________________ outside for a while, when the counselor called him in.
4. "What can I do for you, Jerry?" Mr Reeves asked. "(Wait, *present perfect*) _________________ you _________________________ for long?"

Tipp

Die Wendung 'drop a class' heißt ein Fach abwählen.

5. "Don't worry, sir", Jerry answered. "A problem came up in my mathematics class last week. I (wonder, *present perfect*) ____ ever since, whether I can drop that class and take mathematics again next semester."

Tipp

Die Wendung 'pick on someone' heißt jemanden quälen.

6. "What is the problem?" the counselor wanted to know. "Well", Jerry said, "my mathematics teacher (pick, *present tense*) _________________________ on me all the time."
7. "What happened last week, Jerry? What (do, *past tense*) ____________ you __________________ when it all started?" Mr Reeves wanted to know.

8. Jerry did not know how to put it. But then he said, "I (make, *past tense*) ______________________ faces, and I (imitate, *past perfect*) ______________________ my mathematics teacher for a while when he finally caught me."

9. "Well, Jerry," said Mr Reeves, "why are you surprised? Don't you see that your mathematics teacher (react, *past tense*) ______________________ to your behaviour? I do not think that you behaved as your teacher could have expected."

10. "Now I understand that it was my fault. Next time, I (pay, *future I*) ______________________ attention to what (go, *present tense*) ______________________ on in class. I promise," Jerry said and left Mr Reeve's office.

Überprüfe die Übung mit Hilfe des Lösungsteils.

Verneinung und Fragen

Die **verneinte progressive form** lautet für die **einfachen Zeiten**:

Form von 'be' + not (oder Kurzform von beiden) + *present participle* des Vollverbs (Vollverb + 'ing')

Übung 9 Bilde verneinte Sätze. Benutze die *progressive form* der angegebenen Zeiten.
Form negative sentences and use the progressive form of the given tenses.

Hilfe

Zu den Zeiten lies noch einmal die Seite 29.

1. no, he, not play *(present tense)*

   ______________________________ tennis right now.

2. she, not smile *(past tense)*

   ______________________________ when I saw her.

3. they, not do *(past tense)*

   ______________________________ anything when we entered the room.

Überprüfe die Übung mit Hilfe des Lösungsteils.

Die **verneinte progressive form** lautet für die **Perfektzeiten**:

Form von 'have' + 'not' (oder Kurzform von beiden) +
'been' + *present participle* des Vollverbs (Vollverb + 'ing')
Oder:
'will'/'would' + 'not' (oder Kurzform von beiden) + 'have' +
'been' + *present participle* des Vollverbs (Vollverb + 'ing')

Bilde verneinte Sätze mit der *progressive form* der angegebenen Zeiten.
Form negative sentences and use the progressive form of the given tenses.

Übung 10

1. she, not write *(present perfect)*

   ____

   ______________ for the last five minutes.

2. we, not say *(present perfect)*

   ____

   ______________________ a word.

3. I, not pay *(past perfect)*

   ____

   ________ attention when the teacher called me.

4. they, not sit *(future II)*

   ____

   __________ around for hours as I know them.

5. we, not look *(conditional II)*

   If it had been cloudy, ______________________

   ______________ through the telescope.

Überprüfe die Übung mit Hilfe des Lösungsteils.

Die **verneinte progressive form** lautet für die übrigen zusammengesetzten Zeiten:

'will'/'would' + 'not' (oder Kurzform von beiden) + 'be' + *present participle* des Vollverbs (Vollverb + 'ing')

Übung 11 Bilde verneinte Sätze. Benutze die *progressive form* der angegebenen Zeiten.
Form negative sentences and use the progressive form of the given tenses.

1. I, not climb, mountains, then *(future I)*

____

____.

2. he, not climb, mountains, then *(conditional I)*

He said that _______________________________________

____.

Überprüfe die Übung mit Hilfe des Lösungsteils.

Tipp Zur Bildung der grammatischen Zeiten lies in den klipp & klar Lerntrainern Englisch, 7. und 8. Klasse (rororo 60291 und rororo 60389) nach.

Setze die Verben in die *progressive form*. Benutze jeweils die richtige Zeit.
Put the verbs into the progressive form. Use the right tenses.

Übung 12

1. The car (burn) ______________________ when the police arrived.
2. The driver had been flung out of the car and (lie) ______________________ on the pavement.
3. A woman (try) ______________________ to get help, but she had been unsuccessful before the police arrived.
4. An ambulance and a doctor arrived shortly after the police. "Now they (run) ______________________ over to the man," a girl told another one.
5. "They are quite late," the other girl said, "although they must (drive) ______________________ fast."
6. "True," said the first girl. "And they (go) ______________________ to St. Mary's Hospital at high speed too as soon as they have picked up the man."

Überprüfe die Übung mit Hilfe des Lösungsteils.

So bildest du die **Fragen**:
An der Bildung der **progressive form** ist immer zumindest ein Hilfsverb beteiligt. Die Fragebildung ist daher besonders einfach.

Du bildest die Frage in der **progressive form**, indem du das Subjekt des Aussagesatzes und das (erste) Hilfsverb der **progressive form** miteinander vertauschst. Du bildest die Frage also wie im Deutschen durch einfache Umstellung (Inversion, englisch 'inversion').

Beispiel

1. Aussagesatz: Frage:	**We are** playing a game. **Are we** playing a game?
2. Aussagesatz: Frage:	**The children have** been watching their favourite programme. **Have the children** been watching their favourite programme?
3. Aussagesatz: Frage:	**You will** have been sitting in the hall for a while when the bell rings. **Will you** have been sitting in the hall for a while when the bell rings?

Dasselbe gilt auch für die Umwandlung von negativen Aussagesätzen in Fragen. Beachte aber die Stellung der Verneinungspartikel 'not'.

Benutzt du die **Kurzform 'n't'**, so wird sie an das (erste) Hilfsverb angehängt. Benutzt du die **Vollform 'not'**, so steht diese direkt hinter dem Subjekt der Frage.

Beispiel

1. Aussagesatz: Frage:	**They hadn't** been thinking of it. **Hadn't they** been thinking of it? Oder: **They had not** been thinking of it. **Had they not** been thinking of it?
2. Aussagesatz: Frage:	**The water couldn't** have been dripping. **Couldn't the water** have been dripping? Oder: **The water could not** have been dripping. **Could the water not** have been dripping?

Tipp

Die Vokabel 'drip' heißt tropfen.

Trage ein: *progressive form* oder *simple form*?
Fill in: progressive form or simple form?

Übung 13

1. In August the weather (be) ______________________ better than in April. But, unfortunately, it (rain) ______________________ at the moment.
2. (you, listen) ______________________? I (talk) ______________________ to you.
3. I (get up) ______________________ at half past five every day.
4. Sorry, Ingo cannot come to the phone. He (take) ______________________ a shower right now.
5. Nicole (be) ______________________ in London. She has booked a summer course there.
6. We (not know) ______________________ the results yet. The department heads (still discuss) ______________________ the problem.

Lies vorher noch einmal die Seite 27.

Überprüfe die Übung mit Hilfe des Lösungsteils.

Der Relativsatz

Anwendung

Mit einem **Relativsatz** *(relative clause)* verbindest du zwei Sätze, ohne dich unnötig zu wiederholen.

Beispiel

Im Deutschen könntest du beispielsweise sagen:
Der Hund ist ein nettes Tier.
Der Hund gehört meinem Onkel.
Du kannst dich aber auch besser ausdrücken:
Der Hund, der meinem Onkel gehört, ist ein nettes Tier.

Wenn du Sätze verbindest, ordnest du einen Satz dem anderen Satz unter. Du hast dann einen Hauptsatz *(main clause)* und einen **Relativsatz**. Der **Relativsatz** ist ein erläuternder Nebensatz *(sub-clause)*, der durch ein **Relativpronomen** eingeleitet wird. (Der Hund, **der** …)
Im **Relativsatz** wird immer eine Information aus den ursprünglichen Einzelsätzen verwendet, und zwar die weniger wichtige.

Beispiel

Der Hund ist ein nettes Tier.
Der Hund gehört meinem Onkel.

Die Grundaussage über den Hund soll sein, dass er nett ist.
Die **Grundaussage** steht immer im **Hauptsatz**.
Die Information «gehört meinem Onkel» ist eine Nebeninformation. Sie dient dazu, genau zu bestimmen, um welchen Hund es sich handelt. Die **Nebeninformation** steht immer im **Relativsatz** (Nebensatz).

Der **Relativsatz** erläutert das **Nomen**, das in **beiden** ursprünglichen Sätzen vorkommt. Dies gilt auch, wenn das Nomen im zweiten Satz durch ein Pronomen vertreten wird.

Beispiel

The **girl** is beautiful. The **girl** has red hair.
The **girl** is beautiful. **She** has red hair.
The **girl who has red hair** is beautiful.

Die Relativpronomen

Im Englischen gibt es die folgenden Relativpronomen *(relative pronouns)*: **who, which, that, whose.**
Die Relativpronomen beziehen sich immer auf das vorausgehende Nomen. Dieses Nomen kann im Singular oder im Plural stehen.

Who

Das Relativpronomen 'who' bezieht sich auf Personen.

Tipp

Das Pronomen 'who' enthält ein 'o' und «Personen» enthält ein «o» – 'who' und «Personen» gehören zusammen.

Beispiel

The man wears a green hat. He is our neighbour.

Aus diesen beiden Sätzen kannst du einen Hauptsatz mit einem **Relativsatz** machen. Dies klingt besser:
The man who wears a green hat is our neighbour.

Das Relativpronomen *(relative pronoun)* 'who' bezieht sich auf den vorausgehenden Nominalausdruck 'the man'.

Übung 14 Verbinde jeweils die beiden Sätze. Es sollen immer ein Haupt- und ein Relativsatz entstehen. Benutze 'who'.
Form sentences with a main and a relative clause. Use 'who'.

It is the first day of school after the summer holidays.
Mr Johnson, the new teacher, has to give a lot of instructions.

Beispiel

The girl wears a red T-shirt.
She has to go to the caretaker.
The girl who wears a red T-shirt has to go to the caretaker.

1. The boy has not given back his grammar book.
He has to pay for it.

____

____

2. One of the other teachers taught maths in this class last year.
He will come along in the next lesson.

____

____

____

3. The captain of the football team is looking for a boy.
The boy wants to be a member of this team.

____

____

____

4. The boy wants to leave school.
He goes to see the headmaster.

____

____

Überprüfe die Übung mit Hilfe des Lösungsteils.

In allen Sätzen der Übung 14 werden Haupt- und **Relativsatz** nicht durch Komma abgetrennt, da es sich um **notwendige Relativsätze** handelt.
Ein **Relativsatz** ist notwendig, wenn ohne ihn der Satz nicht eindeutig zu verstehen wäre.

Beispiel

The girl has to go to the caretaker.
Hier ist nicht klar, welches Mädchen gemeint ist.
Steht dagegen ein **Relativsatz**, ist alles klar:
The girl who wears a red T-shirt has to go to the caretaker.

Which

Das Relativpronomen 'which' bezieht sich auf Dinge.

Tipp

Das Relativpronomen 'which' hat ein 'i' und «Dinge» hat ein «i» – 'which' und «Dinge» gehören zusammen.

Beispiel

The pullover belongs to my teacher.
The pullover is out.
Oder besser:
The pullover which belongs to my teacher is out.

Das Relativpronomen *(relative pronoun)* 'which' bezieht sich auf den vorausgehenden Nominalausdruck 'the pullover'.
Im Englischen sind – grammatisch gesehen – auch Tiere Dinge. Im Falle von Haustieren, die einen Namen tragen, wird aber meistens 'who' gebraucht.

Achtung, Stolperstein!

Beispiel

Our cat Sammy, who we bought two years ago, loves chocolates.
Our cat, which we bought two years ago, loves chocolates.

Übung 15 Verbinde jeweils die beiden Sätze. Es sollen immer ein Haupt- und ein Relativsatz entstehen. Benutze 'which'.
Form sentences with a main and a relative clause. Use 'which'.

London

1. The oldest part of London is called 'the City'.
The City is a popular tourist area.

2. St. Paul's Cathedral was built by Sir Christopher Wren.
It is the world's second largest church.

3. One of the most famous buildings in London is the Tower.
The Tower was both, a palace and a prison.

4. Heathrow is one of London's two big airports.
It is one of the most impressive airports in the world.

5. People often visit the Thames Flood Barrier.
The Flood Barrier protects London against floods.

Überprüfe die Übung mit Hilfe des Lösungsteils.

In allen Sätzen der Übung 15 werden Haupt- und **Relativsatz** durch ein Komma voneinander getrennt. Es handelt sich um **nicht notwendige Relativsätze**.
Ein **Relativsatz** heißt «nicht notwendig», wenn der Hauptsatz auch ohne ihn verständlich ist.

Hinweis

Der zweite Satz der Aufgabe 5 von Übung 15 enthält eine Zusatzinformation. Besucher sehen sich die 'Thames Flood Barrier' nicht deshalb an, weil sie London vor einer Flut schützt. Sie besuchen sie, weil sie ein außergewöhnliches, interessantes Bauwerk ist.

Übung 16

Füge 'who' oder 'which' ein.
Insert 'who' or 'which'.

1. The people __________ arrived in America in 1620 were the Pilgrim Fathers.
2. The ship __________ took them to America was called 'Mayflower'.
3. Most of the people __________ left Europe on the 'Mayflower' were Puritans.
4. They had left England __________ was their home country because there they had not been able to practise their religion freely.
5. The hope __________ made them sail to America was the hope of a life in freedom.
6. The voyage, __________ was long and difficult, took two months.
7. The plan __________ the Puritans had agreed upon was that of sailing to Virginia.

Tipp

Die Vokabel 'agreement' heißt Übereinkunft, die Vokabel 'compact' Vertrag, Vereinbarung.

Überprüfe nun deine Lösungen.

8. But shortly before they arrived, they came into a storm ___________ was very strong and ___________ took them to a different part of America.

9. The Puritans on the 'Mayflower' ___________ all felt that they needed some rules in the New World worked out an agreement, the Mayflower Compact.
This agreement, ___________ became their basic law, was signed by every man on board and was the beginning of American democracy.

Verbinde die beiden Sätze jeweils mit 'who' oder 'which'. Entscheide, ob du Haupt- und Relativsatz durch Kommas trennen musst.
Connect the two sentences by 'who' or 'which'. Decide whether or not to use commas.

Übung 17

1. Aunt Barbara will visit us next week.
   She has bought a new car.

   ____

   ____

2. This is the book.
   You were looking for this book.

   ____

   ____

3. The girl really gets on my nerves.
   The girl wears a red dress.

   ____

   ____

4. Sue believes in the existence of the Loch Ness monster.
   She has never seen it.

   ____

   ____

5. Andrew can't remember the name of the boy.
   The boy has red hair.

   ____

   ____

Überprüfe die Übung mit Hilfe des Lösungsteils.

That

In einem **notwendigen Relativsatz** wird statt 'who' oder 'which' häufig 'that' benutzt. 'That' kann sich also auf Personen oder Sachen beziehen.

Hinweis In einem **nicht notwendigen Relativsatz** wird 'that' nicht verwendet.
Nicht vergessen: Der **nicht notwendige Relativsatz** wird immer durch ein Komma abgetrennt.

Übung 18 Entscheide, ob du 'who', 'which' oder 'that' benutzen musst. Gebrauche 'that', wann immer möglich.
Decide whether to use 'who', 'which' or 'that'. Use 'that' whenever possible.

1. One day Mrs Welsh, ____________ had always wanted to go to Paris, decided to do so.
2. She had one secret dream ____________ she had been dreaming for a long time.
3. She had always wanted to have a designer dress ____________ she could wear all by herself when nobody was at home.
4. The money ____________ she needed for such a dress wasn't easy to save, of course.
5. Mrs Welsh, ____________ was a housewife, saw her chance to get some money one day when her neighbour asked her, "Don't you know somebody, ____________ could help me with the housework?"

6. So Mrs Welsh took the job. But she asked her neighbour not to tell her husband, __________ wouldn't have liked the idea.

7. Of course, Mr Welsh would have liked to know what the money was for. But the money __________ Mrs Welsh earned wasn't meant to be for him and the family. It was her money.

8. Her husband, __________ was a hard-working man, __________ liked football very much but would never go to parties, wouldn't have understood her.

9. Mrs Welsh, __________ had never had anything in her life just because it was beautiful, couldn't wait for the day to arrive.

10. But on the day before the trip, __________ she had planned for over 28 years, Mrs Welsh died in an accident.

11. The taxi-driver __________ had killed her said to the police, "She came out of the bank and was smiling. She just ran into the street as if she was dreaming of something."

Überprüfe die Übung mit Hilfe des Lösungsteils.

Das Relativpronomen 'that' musst du nach folgenden Begriffen verwenden:
'all', 'everything', 'something', 'anything', 'nothing'.

Lerne diese Begriffe wie Vokabeln auswendig.

Beispiel

Everything that you did was wrong.
There is still something that I must ask you.

Übung 19 Bilde Sätze und benutze dabei 'who', 'which' oder 'that'.
Form sentences and use 'who', 'which' or 'that'.

1. All __________ I ever wanted was to live a peaceful life.
2. Yesterday I bought the record __________ I have been looking for since it came out.
3. John feels so sick. But he hasn't eaten anything __________ was strange.
4. Sybil wants to buy a pair of jeans in the new shop __________ opened just a week ago.
5. I think that's all __________ I can do for you at the moment.
6. Everything __________ I have done recently seems to be wrong.

Überprüfe die Übung mit Hilfe des Lösungsteils.

Whose

Das Relativpronomen 'whose' zeigt einen Besitz oder eine Zugehörigkeit an.
Es ist der Genitiv der Relativpronomen 'who', 'which' oder 'that'.

Tipp Auf 'whose' folgt immer ein Nomen oder ein Adjektiv + Nomen.
Vor 'whose' steht kein Komma.

Beispiel

The boy whose cat was killed yesterday didn't come to school today.
The car whose old engine broke down is being repaired right now.

Bilde Sätze mit 'whose'.
Form sentences with 'whose'.

Übung 20

Diane's pen-friend Martin from Germany has just arrived. In their letters they have exchanged all sorts of news about Diane's friends. Diane has also sent Martin some photos. Now they are at a party together and Diane tells Martin who is who.

1. You certainly remember Joe. His mother writes detective stories.

 ____

 ____

2. Alan is the boy down there. His father works for the White House.

 ____

 ____

3. I haven't found Mary-Ann yet. Her grandmother never goes out.

 ____

 ____

4. I know you want to meet Jim. His brother is very good at skating.

 ____

 ____

5. But I absolutely want to introduce you to Doreen. Do you remember Doreen? Her guinea pig loves eating candy.

 ____

 ____

 ____

Hinweis

Achte immer darauf, was gemeint ist: 'whose' (dessen) oder 'who's' = 'who is' (wer ist).

Überprüfe die Übung mit Hilfe des Lösungsteils.

Übung 21 Trage ein: 'who' oder 'whose'.
Fill in: 'who' or 'whose'.

Diane continues to introduce people who Martin needs to know.

1. This is our neighbour Mrs Davis, ____________ is a doctor.
2. You remember Francis ____________ father tells such interesting stories about his many travels.
3. The girl ____________ talks to Mrs Davis is Kathleen.
4. Her aunt, ____________ lives in Boston, Massachusetts has invited us for a whole week.
5. That is Francesco ____________ parents own a circus.
6. Andrew is a good person to know. He is someone ____________ you can trust.
7. Who's the lady ____________ car is parked under the no-parking sign?
8. There is a strange competition this year. The boy ____________ is the best cook and the girl ____________ is the best football player will win prizes.
9. The headmaster, ____________ favourite colour is blue, drives a brown Mercedes.
10. The French teacher, ____________ likes poems so much and ____________ English is so good, will travel to Brittany in the summer.

Tipp

'Brittany' ist die englische Bezeichnung für die Bretagne.

Überprüfe die Übung mit Hilfe des Lösungsteils.

Passiv

Anwendung

Das **Passiv** *(passive voice)* benutzt du, wenn dir der Verursacher (Täter, englisch 'agent') einer Handlung unwichtig erscheint oder unbekannt ist. Nun ist die betroffene Person oder der betroffene Gegenstand wichtig. Sie bilden daher das **Subjekt des Passivsatzes.**

Beispiel

The gangster is taken to prison.
The new car has been tested.

Bildung

So bildest du das **Passiv**:

1. Das Verb im Passiv:

Form von 'be' + 3. Form *(past participle)* des Vollverbs

Du setzt das **passivische Verb** in eine bestimmte grammatische Zeit, indem du die Form von 'be' in die betreffende Zeit setzt.

Beispiel

present tense	**am / are / is** injured
past tense	**was / were** injured
present perfect	**has / have been** injured
past perfect	**had been** injured
future I	**will be** injured
future II	**will have been** injured
conditional I	**would be** injured
conditional II	**would have been** injured

Hinweis

Sprichst du über Vorgänge, kannst du das **passivische Verb** statt mit 'be' auch mit 'get' bilden. Diese Formulierung wird häufig noch als umgangssprachlich angesehen.

Beispiel

They stole a CD and **got caught** by the store's detective.

2. Der Passivsatz

Du setzt einen Aktivsatz *(active voice sentence)* ins **Passiv**, indem du zwei Schritte tust:

a) Du setzt das Verb ins **Passiv**.

b) Du stellst Satzglieder des Aktivsatzes um.
Gibt es im Aktivsatz nur ein direktes Objekt *(direct object)*, so wird dies zum **Subjekt des Passivsatzes.**

Beispiel

	Subjekt	Verb	direktes Objekt
Aktivsatz:	They	called	the butler.
Passivsatz:	The butler	was called.	

Das Subjekt des Aktivsatzes wird im Passivsatz nicht mehr erwähnt, wenn es unwichtig ist. Das ist beispielsweise der Fall, wenn das Subjekt ein Pronomen ist oder mit dem deutschen Wort «man» übersetzt werden kann.

Tipp

Ein direktes Objekt ist ein Objekt, auf das die Handlung des Verbs direkt gerichtet ist. Es kann daher einziges Objekt eines Satzes sein. Ein indirektes Objekt *(indirect object)* kann hingegen nur zusammen mit einem direkten Objekt vorkommen.

Hat der Aktivsatz zwei Objekte, ein direktes und ein indirektes, so kann jedes dieser Objekte zum **Subjekt des Passivsatzes** werden. Das indirekte Objekt wird in diesem Fall aber als **Subjekt des Passivsatzes** bevorzugt.

Beispiel

	Subjekt	Verb	indirektes Objekt	direktes Objekt
Aktivsatz:	We	will give	the winner	a prize.
Passivsatz 1:	The winner	will be given		a prize.
Passivsatz 2:	A prize	will be given	to the winner.	
Aktivsatz:	They	sent	their friends	a postcard.
Passivsatz 1:	Their friends	were sent		a postcard.
Passivsatz 2:	A postcard	was sent	to their friends.	
Aktivsatz:	Somebody	has lent	me	a book.
Passivsatz 1:	I	have been lent		a book.
Passivsatz 2:	A book	has been lent	to me.	

Ist das Subjekt des Aktivsatzes eine namentlich bekannte Person oder eine wichtig erscheinende Sache, so kann es im Passivsatz zusätzlich genannt werden. Es wird dann als *by-agent* an den Passivsatz angehängt.

Beispiel

	Subjekt	Verb	Objekt	*by-agent*
Aktivsatz:	Lord Nelson	won	the battle.	
Passivsatz:	The battle	was won		by Lord Nelson.
Aktivsatz:	My dog	bites	the postman.	
Passivsatz:	The postman	is bitten		by my dog.
Aktivsatz:	Sarah	will give	the speech.	
Passivsatz:	The speech	will be given		by Sarah.
Aktivsatz:	The guard	had seen	the thief.	
Passivsatz:	The thief	had been seen		by the guard.
Aktivsatz:	Turner	painted	this picture.	
Passivsatz:	This picture	was painted		by Turner.

Hinweis

Manche Sätze enthalten weitere Satzglieder (beispielsweise Adverbiale des Ortes oder der Zeit). Die weiteren Satzglieder bleiben bei der Umformung (Transformation) des Aktivsatzes in einen Passivsatz (oder umgekehrt) erhalten.

Beispiel

	Adverbiale	Subjekt	Verb	Objekt	*by-agent*
Aktivsatz:	Last night	Susan	kissed	me.	
Passivsatz:	Last night	I	was kissed		by Susan.
Aktivsatz:	Near Hastings	William	defeated	Harold.	
Passivsatz:	Near Hastings	Harold	was defeated		by William.

Bilde passivische Verben in den angegebenen Zeiten.
Form passive voice verb forms in the given tenses.

Übung 22

1. Mary was through with school. All the necessary courses (take, *past perfect*) ________________ .
2. Lots of work (do, *past perfect*) ________________ ________ .
3. It was time for some fun. Her best friends (invite, *past tense*) ________________ to her home for a party.
4. Mary did not want to spend too much money on this party. Therefore a potluck (plan, *past tense*) ________ ________ .
5. 'Potluck' means that food and beverages (bring along, *present tense*) ________________ by the guests.
6. The days before the party are busy days for everyone. Cakes (bake, *present tense*) ________________ , specialties (cook, *present tense*) ________________ and soft drinks (buy, *present tense*) ________________ .
7. Beer, wine and hard drinks (drink, *future I* mit 'cannot') ________________ by people who are not yet 21 years old. That is the law in the USA.
8. After the party, cars (take out, *future I*) ________ ________________ of their garages, and everybody will go cruising in the town center.

Tipp

Die Vokabel 'beverages' heißt Getränke.

Überprüfe die Übung mit Hilfe des Lösungsteils.

Übung 23 Forme Aktivsätze in Passivsätze um. Beachte die Zeiten.
Transform active voice sentences into passive voice sentences. Mind the tenses.

1. They saw her at 8 o'clock in the morning.

2. People have bought hundreds of new stamps.

3. We will move the desk closer to the window.

4. That group will have done the job by noon.

5. People make many mistakes today.

6. They sell flowers every day.

7. People may not pass the border.

Überprüfe die Übung mit Hilfe des Lösungsteils.

Bilde Passivsätze. Entscheide, ob der *by-agent* zu benutzen ist. *Form passive voice sentences. Decide whether or not to use the by-agent.*

Übung 24

1. Sioux Indians attacked General Custer's troops on June 25th, 1876.

____

____

2. They killed all of Custer's men.

____

____

3. People called the incident 'The Battle of the Little Bighorn'.

____

____

4. White Americans regarded the Indians as devils.

____

____

5. Much later, the American government built a monument on the battlefield.

____

____

6. Thousands of tourists visit the monument every year.

____

____

7. They do not see the Indians as devils any more.

____

____

Überprüfe die Übung mit Hilfe des Lösungsteils.

Du kannst das **Passiv** auch von Verben bilden, auf die eine Präposition folgt. Die Präposition steht auch bei der Umformung vom Aktiv ins Passiv **immer direkt hinter** dem Vollverb.

Beispiel

to laugh at	The boy **was laughed at** by his friends.
to look into	The problem **has been looked into** by experts.
to think of	The singer **will be thought of** highly one day.
to look after	The children **were looked after** by a baby sitter.
to agree to	Before the plan was carried out, it **had been agreed to** by the Queen.

Schließlich kannst du auch das *present progressive* und das *past progressive* in das **Passiv** setzen. In den übrigen grammatischen Zeiten ist das **Passiv** der *progressive form* unüblich.

Beispiel

present progressive, passive voice
The Last Night of the Proms **is being brought** to you by the BBC.

past progressive, passive voice
When I came in, I heard that a speech **was being given** by the headmaster.

Wiederholungsübungen

1. Wiederholung

Jetzt hast du zwei Wochen Pause. Trage das Datum des Tages, an dem du mit den Wiederholungsübungen anfangen wirst (heute in zwei Wochen), in die Tabelle «1. Wiederholung» und in deinen Kalender (oder den deiner Eltern) ein. Hake dann alle Übungen, die du erledigt hast, nach und nach in der Tabelle ab. Überprüfe anschließend deine Lösungen.

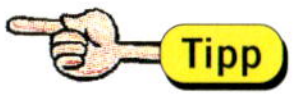

Hast du dir schon das Kapitel «Der Vokabeltrainer» (auf den Seiten 79–84) durchgelesen? Hier erhältst du Tipps, die es dir erleichtern, Vokabeln zu lernen und zu behalten.

Bearbeite pro Tag zwei Übungen.

1. Wiederholung Beginn: ______			
Der Artikel W 1.1	Die 'progressive form' W 1.2	Der Relativsatz W 1.3	Das Passiv W 1.4

W 1.1 Entscheide, ob du ‘a’ oder ‘an’ einsetzen musst oder nicht.
Decide whether or not to use ‘a’ or ‘an’.

1. Last year we went on __a__ trip to the United States.
2. We travelled about 200 miles __a__ day.
3. We flew to New York and then we rented __an__ expensive car.
4. We first went to __a__ Chicago where we met __a__ friend of my dad’s.
5. He is __a__ dentist just as my dad is, and both studied in Freiburg.
6. His name is Mike. Mike’s father was __a__ soldier, and so the whole family lived in Germany. But they went home to America once __a__ year.
7. Mike told us that they visited two to three relatives __a__ week just to keep in __a__ contact when they were in the States.
8. Well, after that we decided to drive to Minneapolis where my Mum has __a__ friend.
9. She is __a__ policewoman, just as my Mum.
10. The problem was that she is __a__ Muslim and that when we arrived they celebrated Ramadan.
11. Muslims do so once __a__ year.
12. We stayed with my Mum’s friend and her family. They were such ______ nice people.

13. Mum's friend Yasmin told us that as ___a___ girl she did not like Ramadan because at that time Muslims cannot eat during the day.

14. And she loved ___a___ Christian holiday, Christmas, so much.

15. Once ___a___ girl-friend had invited her for ___a___ Christmas, and she was allowed to take part in the holiday.

16. Yasmin told us what ___an___ exciting event it had been for her.

17. Well, we travelled quite ___a___ lot but those two visits were the best ones because we came to know real ______ Americans who had been in contact with our family for ___a___ long time.

Überprüfe die Übung mit Hilfe des Lösungsteils.

W 1.2 Bilde bejahte und verneinte Aussagesätze und Fragen. Benutze die *progressive form* in den angegebenen Zeiten.
Schreibe die Sätze in dein Heft.
Form positive (affirmative) and negative statements and questions. Use the progressive form in the given tenses. Write the sentences into your notebook.

1. one day, Professor Know-All, think *(past tense)* of a
   wonderful new machine,
   when Mr Smart came to visit him
2. Professor Know-All asked his guest to sit down.
   Soon, they, have *(past tense)*, tea
3. Mr Smart asked his host,
   "what, you, work on *(present perfect)*?"
4. Professor Know-All, think about *(past perfect)*,
   a new toy for children.
5. but, he, not go *(past tense)*,
   to tell Mr Smart about it
6. Professor Know-All thought,
   "tomorrow, I, develop *(future I)*,
   a new automatic bird that can fly and sing.
7. In the middle of my work, Little Georgie will come over
   and ask me for a toy.
   he, not sit still *(future I)*, in my lab
8. he, jump around *(future I)*, even more,
   when I will give him the new toy
   that I, go *(present tense)* to call 'Hootchy-kootchy'."

Tipp

Die Vokabel 'host' heißt Gastgeber.

Überprüfe die Übung mit Hilfe des Lösungsteils.

Setze das richtige Relativpronomen ein: 'who', 'which', 'that', 'whose'. W 1.3

Put in the correct relative pronoun: 'who', 'which', 'that', 'whose'.

Talking about teachers

1. Robert, "I wonder whether the new gentleman over there is the one __________ will teach maths in our class in the next term."
2. Janet, "No, that is Mr Green. Our new maths teacher is probably the one __________ is never really prepared for school."
3. Mike, "Oh, no. You think of the one __________ car constantly breaks down and __________ is always late for school."
4. Ronny, "Clive __________ father is the headmaster told me yesterday that Mr Dragon might be our maths teacher."
5. Robert, "Mr Dragon! That sounds fantastic. By the way, did you know that there will be a new pupil? That is something __________ I don't like. We are already 33 pupils!"
6. Janet, "That's right. We don't need someone __________ is going to be number 34."
7. Mike, "Don't be so stupid. One more doesn't change anything. All __________ can be said right now is that the new one is number 34."
8. Ronny, "But there isn't anything __________ we can do."
9. Janet, "I only hope that the new one __________ you are talking of is a girl!"

Überprüfe die Übung mit Hilfe des Lösungsteils.

W 1.4 Bilde Passivsätze. Beachte die angegebenen Zeiten.
Form passive voice sentences. Mind the given tenses.

1. The Musical Company did the 'West Side Story'.

2. People had eaten breakfast.

3. We were reading the dialogue.

4. Jimmy read the short story.

5. They will have repeated the unit before the testing day.

Tipp
Die Vokabel 'shooting star' heißt Sternschnuppe.

6. Karen and Billy have seen several shooting stars.

7. Werner is running the London marathon.

8. I have done a good job on this exercise.

Überprüfe die Übung mit Hilfe des Lösungsteils.

2. Wiederholung

ELTERN Hilfe

Jetzt hast du die «1. Wiederholung» beendet. Du hast nun vier Wochen Pause. Trage das Datum des Tages, an dem du mit der «2. Wiederholung» anfangen wirst (heute in vier Wochen), unten in die Tabelle und in deinen Kalender (oder den deiner Eltern) ein. Verfahre dann genauso wie bei der 1. Wiederholung.

Arbeite in deiner Lernkartei (siehe Seite 80–84) weiter.

Tipp

Bearbeite pro Tag zwei Übungen.

2. Wiederholung	Beginn: ______________		
Der Artikel W 2.1	**Die 'progressive form'** W 2.2	**Der Relativsatz** W 2.3	**Das Passiv** W 2.4

Tipp

Die Wendung 'to be articulate' heißt redegewandt sein.

W 2.1 Schreibe mit Hilfe der Wörter einen Text in dein Heft. Achte darauf, ob du einen bestimmten oder unbestimmten Artikel benutzen musst oder nicht.
Write a text with the help of the given words into your notebook. Pay attention to whether or not to use an article.

1. Uncle John – be – musician.
2. He often – go to – concerts – but he – love – all – concerts that – be given in – churches.
3. church – he – like – most – be – St. Anna's Church.
4. He – think – acoustics – be best – there.
5. Uncle John – play – piano – and – cello.
6. He – play – piano – with – his friend Roberto – who – be – doctor – and – he – play – flute – with – his friend Pierre – who be – hairdresser.
7. Roberto – be – Italian – and Pierre – be – Frenchman.
8. Roberto – be quite – good – friend of Uncle John's.
9. Twice – week – they – meet and play together.
10. Most of – time – they – play Mozart.
11. Uncle John – say – that – most musicians – love Mozart.
12. He is rather – expert – on Mozart.
13. He – say – that – life – more interesting – if – you – love – music.
14. Art – make – you – always happy.

Überprüfe die Übung mit Hilfe des Lösungsteils.

Entscheide: *progressive form* oder *simple form*?
Decide: progressive form or simple form?

W 2.2

1. You may have heard of Chief Seattle, an Indian chief who (live) ______________ in the Pacific Northwest in the 19th century. An important city got his name.
2. People say that one day, when Chief Seattle (travel) ______________ around in what is now Western Washington, he (get) ______________ angry with the Whites.
3. "It is a fact that Whites (not make) ______________ use of trees, fish and game as they should," Seattle said.
4. "This morning I saw someone who (cut) ______________ the two best pieces of meat from some deer. Later, he (leave) ______________ the larger part of the deer behind."
5. Then, people say, Chief Seattle (write) ______________ a letter to the Whites. 'You (abuse) ______________ nature. Stop this!' the letter says.
6. But this (be) ______________ only a story that (be) ______________ made up in Hollywood.
7. As a real Indian, Chief Seattle tried to preserve nature. But he (not write) ______________ letters.
8. He was not a modern man. One day when whites (photograph) ______________ him, he closed his eyes. He thought that the camera would take his soul out of his body, right through his eyes.

Tipp

Die Vokabel 'game' heißt hier Wild.

Überprüfe die Übung mit Hilfe des Lösungsteils.

W 2.3 Setze das richtige Relativpronomen ein: 'who', 'which', 'that', 'whose'.
Fill in the correct relative pronoun: 'who', 'which', 'that', 'whose'.

Tipp Die Vokabel 'rabies' heißt Tollwut.

Rabies

1. Britons, __________ generally love animals a lot, are afraid of rabies.
2. People __________ want to take their animal along can't spend their holidays in Britain.
3. It is forbidden to take animals, __________ , of course, are often people's best friends, into Britain without permission.
4. Everything regarding animals __________ is no problem in other European countries seems to be a problem in Britain.
5. Even if you have got permission, there is something __________ you have to do. You have to leave your animal in quarantine for six months.
6. This might seem very hard for you and your animal but it is a rule __________ you have to follow.
7. After these six months, __________ might seem long to you and your animal, you are allowed to take your pet home.
8. People __________ try to smuggle their pets into the country will be in great trouble.
9. The customs officers __________ job it is to look for animals will have to take smuggled animals away and kill them.

Überprüfe die Übung mit Hilfe des Lösungsteils.

Bilde Passivsätze. Beachte die angegebenen Zeiten.
Form passive voice sentences. Mind the given tenses.

W 2.4

1. The art teacher is looking at pupils' drawings.

2. The police arrested seven photographers.

3. They could have arrested three more of them.

4. Spiders eat flies and other small insects.

5. Yesterday Sir Yehudi Menuhin conducted the London Symphony Orchestra.

6. Grade 13 will visit Dublin.

7. They had seen London before.

Überprüfe die Übung mit Hilfe des Lösungsteils.

Eine gute Vorbereitung: Tests zum Üben

Hinweis

Hier einige Tipps, die dir zugleich helfen, bessere Klassenarbeiten zu schreiben.

Nicht gleich anfangen! Wenn der Aufgabenzettel ausgeteilt ist, solltest du auf keinen Fall sofort zu arbeiten beginnen, sonst gehen dir vielleicht wichtige mündliche Hinweise verloren, die der Lehrer gibt. Solche Hinweise schreibst du nicht auf irgendeinen Zettel, sondern gleich auf das Aufgabenblatt.

Alles durchlesen! Lies die Aufgabenstellung sorgfältig Wort für Wort durch und markiere mit dem Farbstift wichtige Stellen des Arbeitsauftrages. Bei jeder Aufgabe solltest du genau überlegen: Was ist gegeben – was ist verlangt?

Einfälle sofort stichwortartig notieren! Was dir bereits beim Lesen zur Aufgabenlösung einfällt, notiere gleich auf dem Blatt neben der Aufgabe – und zwar leserlich.

Die Zeit einteilen! Teile die Zeit entsprechend der Anzahl der Aufgaben ein. Solltest du innerhalb der geplanten Zeit die Aufgabe nicht lösen können, fange mit der nächsten an.

Vom Leichten zum Schweren! Bearbeite erst die Aufgaben, die du auf Anhieb lösen kannst; dann legt sich deine Aufregung.

Genau abschreiben! Wenn du z. B. Verben ins Passiv setzen sollst, passieren leicht Rechtschreibfehler. Das kann schon einen Punktabzug bedeuten.

Eine Probe machen! Das fertige Ergebnis solltest du noch einmal überprüfen. Vergleiche deine Lösung mit der Fragestellung der Aufgabe. Stellst du dabei fest, dass Wesentliches fehlt oder falsch ist, kannst du wenigstens noch kurz angeben, wie die Lösung aussehen könnte. Falsches streichst du durch.

Tipp

Solch ein Test macht ungefähr ein Drittel einer Klassenarbeit aus. Siehe auch Seite 9.

Für die Tests in diesem Band hast du 15 Minuten Zeit. Arbeite bitte nicht länger, damit du eine realistische Einschätzung deines Arbeitstempos bekommst. Am Ende der einzelnen Tests erfährst du, wie du deine Gesamtpunktzahl und deine Zensur ermittelst.

Test 1: Der Artikel

Zeit: 15 Minuten

Entscheide, ob du 'the', 'a' oder 'an' einsetzen musst.
Decide whether to fill in 'the', 'a', 'an'.

Conversation in a pub

1. Robert Mc Court, "Did you know that John is ________ Catholic, too?"
2. Bill Mc Allistair, "I always thought he was ________ Protestant, because he never goes to ________ church."
3. Robert Mc Court, "I only saw him once at ________ church that I go to. Besides, did you know that John is in ________ hospital right now?"
4. Bill Mc Allistair, "No, I didn't know that. Let's go to ________ hospital and visit him. Do you think we should give him ________ flowers, or a bottle of whiskey?"
5. Robert Mc Court, "By the way, do you remember ________ whiskey we bought when we travelled through Scotland by bike? We often travelled 50 miles ________ day. Sometimes we did 40 miles in half ________ day."
6. Bill Mc Allistair, "Yes, I was ________ paper boy then. And I had only 15 days of vacation

_______ year. We used the holidays for our bike tours. As _______ paper boy I earned only £ 4 _______ week."

7. Robert Mc Court, "As _______ youngster you never earned much those days. But nevertheless I like to think of the old days. What _______ good time we had. But what is best, you are still quite _______ good friend."

Überprüfe Test 1 mit Hilfe des Lösungsteils.

Bewertung

Du kannst insgesamt 17 Punkte erreichen. Pro Fehler musst du einen Punkt abziehen. Rechne nun die Punkte zusammen und ermittle deine Note. Ich habe ☐ von 17 Punkten.

Punkte	17–16	15–14	13–12	11–10	9–8	7–0
Zensur	1	2	3	4	5	6

Nach diesem Bewertungsmaßstab kannst du deine Leistungen einschätzen.

Test 2: Die 'progressive form'

Zeit:
15 Minuten

Bilde bejahte und verneinte Aussagesätze und Fragen. Benutze die *progressive form* in den angegebenen Zeiten.
Form positive (affirmative) and negative statements and questions. Use the progressive form in the given tenses.

Mr Smart had talked Professor Know-All into selling him the new toy 'Hootchy-kootchy'.

1. Mr Smart said,
   "I, sit *(present tense)*, here, and I, talk *(present tense)*,
   to you.
2. I, call (*conditional I*: sollte), my business partner
   and tell him what I bought."
3. Professor Know-All was astonished and asked,
   "you, go *(present tense)*,
   to produce thousands of 'Hootchy-kootchies'?
4. I thought that you bought the toy for your son.
   What, I, dream *(past tense)*, of?"
5. Mr Smart, smile *(past tense)*,
   when he heard that.
6. Professor Know-All understood
   that he, not pay *(past perfect)*, attention.
   He had signed a paper. It must have been a contract.
7. When the professor, throw *(past tense)*, him out,
   Mr Smart said, "It has been nice to do business with you,
   Professor."

Überprüfe Test 2 mit Hilfe des Lösungsteils.

Bewertung

Du kannst insgesamt 19 Punkte erreichen. Pro richtig gebildete *progressive form* erhältst du 2 Punkte. Für richtig gebildete Fragen und für das richtig gestellte 'not' in Satz 6 gibt es jeweils einen Punkt extra.
Rechne nun die Punkte zusammen und ermittle deine Note.

Ich habe ☐ von 19 Punkten.

Punkte	19–18	17–16	15–13	12–11	10–9	8–0
Zensur	1	2	3	4	5	6

Nach diesem Bewertungsmaßstab kannst du deine Leistungen einschätzen.

Test 3: Die Relativpronomen

Zeit:
15 Minuten

Setze das richtige Relativpronomen ein: 'who', 'which', 'that', 'whose'.
Fill in the correct relative pronoun: 'who', 'which', 'that', 'whose'.

1. Winston's uncle, __________ has a Ferrari, is sometimes invited by the Ferrari people for a Ferrari festival, __________ always takes place in Italy.
2. Anything __________ has to do with cars is most exciting for Winston.
3. The cars __________ he likes most are British cars.
4. So he adores the Rolls-Royce and the Bentley, __________ of course are most expensive cars.
5. He finds that there is nothing __________ can interest boys more than cars.
6. This year Winston's uncle, __________ in fact is quite rich, has invited Winston to go with him to Italy to the Ferrari meeting.
7. Winston __________ father also is in love with cars understands him and has allowed him to accompany his uncle.
8. Winston's mother, __________ is his uncle's sister and __________ knows that her brother likes driving quickly, is a bit afraid.
9. Nevertheless she as well has allowed Winston to accompany his uncle, __________ promised to drive carefully.

10. So they both prepared the trip, __________ should become an exciting one.

11. Winston __________ task it was to wash the Ferrari before the trip did everything __________ he could do to please his uncle.

12. He even worked out a route __________ he thought would take them through the most interesting areas of Europe. And finally the big day was there.

Überprüfe Test 3 mit Hilfe des Lösungsteils.

Bewertung

Du kannst insgesamt 15 Punkte erreichen. Pro Fehler musst du einen Punkt abziehen. Rechne nun die Punkte zusammen und ermittle deine Note. Ich habe ☐ von 15 Punkten.

Punkte	15–14	13–12	11–10	9–8	7–6	5–0
Zensur	1	2	3	4	5	6

Nach diesem Bewertungsmaßstab kannst du deine Leistungen einschätzen.

Test 4: Das Passiv

Bilde Passivsätze. Beachte die gegebenen Zeiten.
Form passive voice sentences. Mind the given tenses.

Zeit: 15 Minuten

1. They gave the winner a gold medal.

   a) ______________________________

   b) ______________________________

2. The chairperson will lead tomorrow's discussions.

   ____

   ____

3. Storm and heavy rain stopped all air traffic.

   ____

   ____

4. We were giving a lot of applause.

   ____

   ____

5. People would have informed all the neighbours.

   ____

   ____

6. Thomas' parents have not informed the school about the child's absence.

   ____

   ____

   ____

Hinweis

In der ersten Aufgabe gibt es zwei Umformungsmöglichkeiten.

Tipp

Die Vokabel 'chairperson' heißt Vorsitzende(r).

Überprüfe Test 4 mit Hilfe des Lösungsteils.

Bewertung

Du kannst insgesamt 22 Punkte erreichen. Pro richtige Verbform erhältst du 2 Punkte. Du erhältst außerdem je einen Punkt für den richtigen Satzbau und für den *by-agent*. Hast du einen *by-agent* gewählt, obwohl keiner benutzt werden sollte, musst du einen Punkt abziehen.

Rechne nun die Punkte zusammen und ermittle deine Note.

Ich habe ☐ von 22 Punkten.

Punkte	22–21	20–18	17–15	14–12	11–9	8–0
Zensur	1	2	3	4	5	6

Nach diesem Bewertungsmaßstab kannst du deine Leistungen einschätzen.

Der Vokabeltrainer

Wenn man schon nicht drum herumkommt ...

Die folgenden Tipps helfen dir, Vokabeln leichter zu lernen und langfristig zu behalten.

Stufe I zeigt dir, wie du für die nächste Stunde lernst.
Sobald das klappt, auf zur Stufe II.
Stufe II zeigt dir, wie du die Vokabeln auch noch nach einem halben Jahr weißt.
Sobald das eine gute Gewohnheit ist, belebt Abwechslung das Pauken. Auf zur Stufe III.
Stufe III zeigt dir, dass Üben auch ganz anders geht: zeichnen, kleben und spielen.

Hinweis

Wenn du dir die Vokabeln für die nächste Stunde bereits ohne Mühe merkst, kannst du gleich die Tipps für die Stufe II lesen und regelmäßig anwenden.

Stufe I: «Lernt bis übermorgen die Vokabeln der Lektion 7.»
So gehst du vor.

1. Sieh dir gleich am Nachmittag die Vokabeln an. Dabei stellst du fest, dass du einige Wörter schnell lernen kannst, weil sie fast genauso wie die deutschen Wörter aussehen ('house' oder 'finger').
2. Lerne immer sieben Vokabeln auf einmal. Sieben prägen sich rasch ein. Der Vokabelberg wird schnell kleiner.
3. Kreuze die «schweren Brocken» an und schreibe sie auf. Durch das Aufschreiben gehst du besonders aufmerksam mit diesen sperrigen Vokabeln um.
4. Nun hast du schon prima gearbeitet. Gehe jetzt noch einmal alle Vokabeln durch und überprüfe, welche du schon kannst. Fertig. Erst einmal sacken lassen.
5. Gegen Abend fragst du dich erneut die Vokabeln ab. Die Reihe der englischen Wörter zudecken. Ein deutsches Wort heraussuchen. Die englische Übersetzung sagen, kontrollieren. Die nicht gekonnten Begriffe wieder aufschreiben.

6. Am nächsten Tag stellst du fest, was noch nicht sitzt. Schreibe immer sieben dieser Vokabeln auf Kärtchen oder einen kleinen Zettel und lerne sie Zettel für Zettel.
7. Gegen Abend lässt du dich abfragen.

Stufe II: Sicher gewusst – auch noch nach einem halben Jahr

Damit dein Gehirn weiß, was wichtig ist, braucht es die Wiederholung. Das bewährte Mittel ist die Lernkartei. Sie besteht aus Kärtchen, die auf der einen Seite die englische Vokabel und einen typischen Beispielsatz enthalten. Du findest ihn in dem dreispaltigen Wörterverzeichnis deines Lehrbuches. In diesem Satz ist das zu lernende Wort durch eine Umschreibung ersetzt. Auf der Rückseite des Kärtchens stehen das deutsche Wort und die Übersetzung des Beispielsatzes.

Tipp

Unterstreiche im englischen Beispielsatz die zum Verb gehörenden Präpositionen (z. B. 'by').

Beispiel

fare The money that you pay to go by bus, train or ship.	**Fahrgeld** Das Geld, das man bezahlt, um mit dem Bus, dem Zug oder dem Schiff zu fahren.

Die Lernkartei	
Start am ersten Tag 1. Schritt (nachmittags)	Beschrifte als Erstes 7 Vokabelkarten (DIN A7): Schreibe die Vokabel und einen Beispielsatz auf die Vorderseite und die deutsche Übersetzung auf die Rückseite. **Lerne** nun diese Vokabeln. Jede *gekonnte* Karte kommt ins Fach 2. Jede *nicht gekonnte* Karte kommt ins Fach 1.
2. Schritt (abends)	**Wiederhole** alle Karten aus den Fächern 1 und 2. Die *gekonnten* Karten wandern ein Fach weiter, also in die Fächer 2 und 3. Jede *nicht gekonnte* Karte kommt ins Fach 1.

In der Woche (Montag, Dienstag, Mittwoch, Donnerstag) 1. Schritt (nachmittags)	**Wiederhole** alle Karten aus den Fächern 1, 2 und 3. Die *gekonnten* Karten wandern ein Fach weiter, also in die Fächer 2, 3 und 4. Jede *nicht gekonnte* Karte kommt ins Fach 1. Beschrifte 7 neue Kärtchen. **Lerne** nun diese Vokabeln. Jede *gekonnte* Karte kommt ins Fach 2. Jede *nicht gekonnte* Karte kommt ins Fach 1.
2. Schritt (abends)	**Wiederhole** alle Karten aus den Fächern 1 und 2. Die *gekonnten* Karten wandern ein Fach weiter, also in die Fächer 2 und 3. Jede *nicht gekonnte* Karte kommt ins Fach 1.
Jedes Wochenende (Freitag, Samstag oder Sonntag)	**Wiederhole** alle Karten aus dem Fach 4. Jede *gekonnte* Karte kommt ins Fach 5. Jede *nicht gekonnte* Karte kommt ins Fach 1.
Nach einem Monat	**Wiederhole** alle Karten aus dem Fach 5. Jede *gekonnte* Karte kommt ins Fach 6. Jede *nicht gekonnte* Karte kommt ins Fach 1.
Jeweils in den Ferien	**Wiederhole** alle Karten aus dem Fach 6. Jede *gekonnte* Karte wird aussortiert.* Jede *nicht gekonnte* Karte kommt ins Fach 1.

* Nach einem Halbjahr ist der Kasten voll. Sortiere alle Karten alphabetisch, dann hast du ein eigenes Wörterbuch. Fange einen neuen Kasten an.

Hast du zu Hause einen Computer, kannst du mit einem Vokabelprogramm genauso regelmäßig üben. Diese Programme arbeiten wie die Lernkartei.

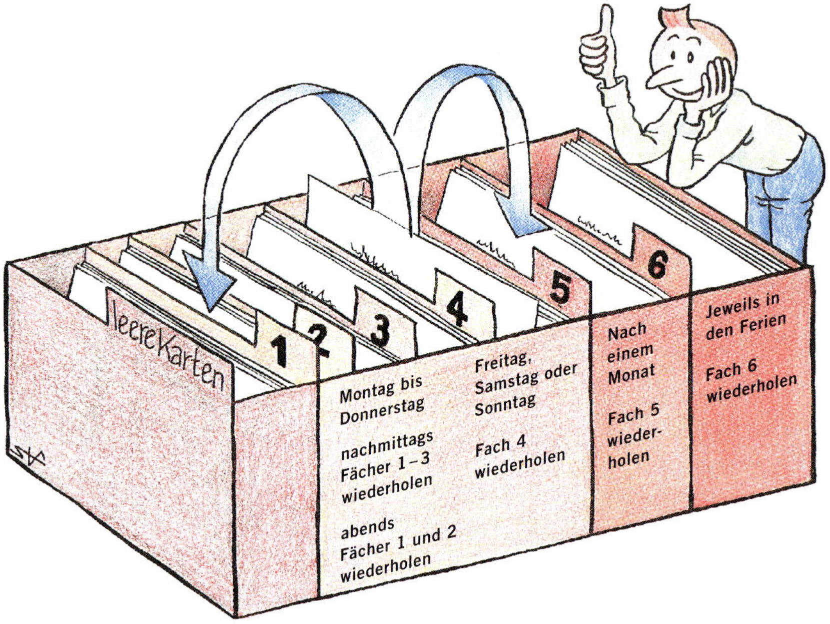

Stufe III: Wiederholung muss sein – Langeweile nicht

Damit gelernte Vokabeln nicht einzeln (unverbunden) in deinem Kopf umherschwirren, musst du sie ordnen. Auch deine Socken findest du schneller, wenn dein Schrank aufgeräumt ist.
Hierzu gibt es mehrere Alternativen:

- Zeichne dir eine Gedächtnislandkarte (eine Mindmap). Schreibe auf Englisch in die Mitte eines DIN-A4-Blattes ein Thema, das dich interessiert (z. B. 'That's me' oder 'At a disco'). Notiere zunächst Hauptpunkte, die du dann in Einzelheiten unterteilst. Fehlt dir ein englisches Wort, schreibe erst einmal das deutsche Wort auf. Tausche am Schluss alle deutschen Begriffe gegen die englischen Vokabeln aus (Lexikon benutzen). Die Gedächtnislandkarte prägt sich noch besser ein, wenn du Begriffe durch Bilder ergänzt. Du kannst sie selber zeichnen oder aus Illustrierten ausschneiden. (Siehe Beispiel Seite 84.)

- Lege dir ein Vokabelringbuch an.
  Auf die Registerblätter schreibst du Themen, die dich interes-

sieren oder die gerade im Unterricht behandelt werden, z. B. 'my room', 'sports', 'clothes', 'hobbies'.
Auf den Seiten hinter dem Registerblatt sammelst du zu jedem Begriff passende Ausdrücke und Redewendungen. Versuche dabei, nach und nach bestimmte sprachliche Gruppen zu bilden:

- gegensätzliche Adjektive,
- sinn- und sachverwandte Wörter,
- idiomatische Wendungen, also typische Redewendungen (während es bei uns «Bindfäden regnet», regnet es in England 'cats and dogs'),
- Präpositionen.

Teile dir zum Lernen Siebenergruppen ein.

– Mache **spielerisch** weiter.
Schreibe auf die Vorderseite von grünen Kärtchen englische Vokabeln und auf die jeweilige Rückseite ein englisches Wort mit gleicher bzw. ähnlicher Bedeutung. Schreibe auf die Vorderseite von roten Kärtchen englische Vokabeln und auf die jeweilige Rückseite ein englisches Wort mit gegensätzlicher Bedeutung.
Spielregeln: Die Kärtchen liegen zu Beginn auf einem Stapel. Reihum nennt jeder Spieler den Gegenbegriff (mit ähnlicher oder gegensätzlicher Bedeutung) zu dem sichtbaren Wort. Wer diese Aufgabe richtig gelöst hat, erhält die Karte. Bei falscher Antwort kommt die Karte wieder unter den Stapel. Sieger ist, wer am Ende die meisten Karten hat.

– Benutze einen **Kniff** der alten Griechen.
Schreibe alle Vokabeln, die nicht in den Kopf wollen, auf kleine Haftzettel. Verteile diese dann an Stellen in der Wohnung, an denen du oft vorbeigehst. Jedes Mal, wenn du an ihnen vorbeikommst, wirfst du einen Blick auf die Zettel – mehr nicht. So verbinden sich bestimmte Orte mit bestimmten Wörtern. Gehst du später in Gedanken die Wegstrecke ab, tauchen auch die Wörter wieder auf.

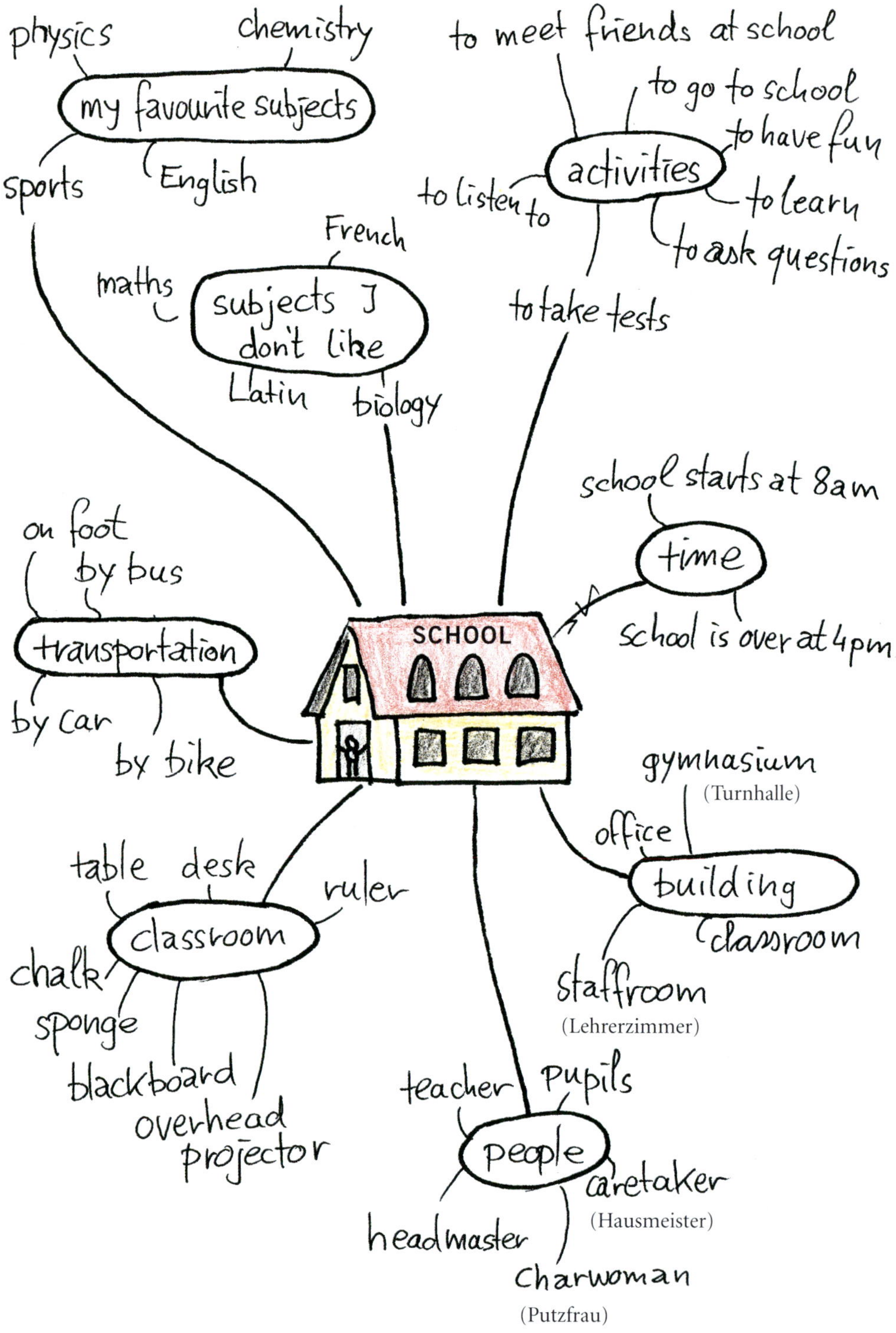
physics
chemistry
my favourite subjects
sports
English
to meet friends at school
to go to school
to have fun
activities
to listen to
to learn
to ask questions
to take tests
French
maths
subjects I don't like
Latin
biology
school starts at 8am
time
school is over at 4pm
on foot
by bus
transportation
by car
by bike
SCHOOL
gymnasium
(Turnhalle)
office
building
classroom
staffroom
(Lehrerzimmer)
table
desk
ruler
classroom
chalk
sponge
blackboard
overhead projector
teacher
pupils
people
caretaker
(Hausmeister)
headmaster
charwoman
(Putzfrau)

Zum Vergleichen: Die Lösungen

Der Artikel

Lösungen zu Übung 1

Seite 12

1. **The** society; **the** society
2. society, life, all **the** time
3. **the** buses, buses
4. **The** bus
5. **the** water, **the** meat
6. water, meat
7. most people, meat
8. Most of **the** young people, panicking

Lösungen zu Übung 2

Seite 14

1. go to **the** church
2. went to church
3. leave school, left school, went to university
4. go to hospital, go to **the** hospital
5. meet at **the** cinema, go to **the** church
6. go to school

Lösungen zu Übung 3

Seite 16

1. play **the** piano
2. playing **the** piano, playing **the** violin
3. **the** piano and **the** violin
4. all **the** afternoon
5. all **the** Monday afternoons
6. All **the** Saturdays
7. go to Hyde Park
8. see Buckingham Palace, **the** Tower, **the** Thames Flood Barrier, **the** Houses of Parliament, St. Paul's Cathedral

Lösungen zu Übung 4

Seite 18

1. a	8. an
2. a	9. an
3. an	10. a
4. an	11. an
5. an	12. an
6. a	13. an
7. a	14. an

Radiere falsche Lösungen aus. Bearbeite diese Aufgaben noch einmal.

Seite 19 Lösungen zu Übung 5

1. an	9. an
2. a	10. a
3. an	11. a
4. a	12. an
5. a	13. an
6. an	14. a
7. an	15. an
8. an	

Tipp **Hast du daran gedacht, dir die Wörter vorzusprechen? So hörst du, ob sie mit einem Vokal oder Konsonanten anlauten.**

Seite 21 Lösungen zu Übung 6

1. become **a** doctor, become **a** farmer, is **a** judge, I'm **a** dentist, don't have farmers, become **a** farmer
2. be **an** ambulance driver, is **a** reporter
3. be **an** ice-skater
4. what **a** wonderful dentist

Seite 23 Lösungen zu Übung 7

1. What **a** surprise, found **a** cheque
2. once **a** month
3. have **a** grandma
4. What **a** problem
5. You know life, as **a** teenager
6. 80p **a** glass, 50p **a** cup, £ 40 **a** pair
7. what life was like, as **a** young girl
8. was **a** young girl

Die 'progressive form'

Seite 30 Lösungen zu Übung 8

1. Jerry came into the counselor's office when Mr Ken Reeves, the counselor, **was talking** on the phone.
2. Jerry, I **am talking** to a parent right now.
3. Jerry **had been sitting** outside for a while, when the counselor called him in.
4. **Have** you **been waiting** for long?
5. I **have been wondering** ever since, whether I can drop that class and take mathematics again next semester.
6. Well, my mathematics teacher **is picking** on me all the time.
7. What **were** you **doing** when it all started?
8. I **was making** faces, and I **had been imitating** my mathematics teacher for a while when he finally caught me.
9. Don't you see that your mathematics teacher **was reacting** to your behaviour?
10. Next time, I **will be paying** attention to what **is going** on in class.

Lösungen zu Übung 9 Seite 32

1. **No, he isn't (is not) playing** tennis right now.
2. **She wasn't (was not) smiling** when I saw her.
3. **They weren't (were not) doing** anything when we entered the room.

Lösungen zu Übung 10 Seite 33

1. **She hasn't (has not) been writing** for the last five minutes.
2. **We haven't (have not) been saying** a word.
3. **I hadn't (had not) been paying** attention when the teacher called me.
4. **They won't (will not) have been sitting** around for hours as I know them.
5. If it had been cloudy, we **wouldn't (would not) have been looking** through the telescope.

Lösungen zu Übung 11 Seite 34

1. I won't (will not) be climbing mountains then.
2. He said that **he wouldn't (would not) be climbing mountains then.**

Lösungen zu Übung 12 Seite 35

1. was burning
2. was lying
3. had been trying
4. are running
5. must have been driving
6. will be going

Lösungen zu Übung 13 Seite 37

1. is, is raining
2. Are you listening? I am talking to you.
3. get up
4. is taking
5. is
6. don't (do not) know, are still discussing

Der Relativsatz

Lösungen zu Übung 14 Seite 40

1. The boy who has not given back his grammar book has to pay for it.
2. One of the other teachers who taught maths in this class last year will come along in the next lesson.
3. The captain of the football team is looking for a boy who wants to be a member of this team.
4. The boy who wants to leave school goes to see the headmaster.

Radiere falsche Lösungen aus. Bearbeite diese Aufgaben noch einmal.

Seite 42 Lösungen zu Übung 15

1. The oldest part of London, which is a popular tourist area, is called 'the City'.
2. St. Paul's Cathedral, which is the world's second largest church, was built by Sir Christopher Wren.
3. One of the most famous buildings in London is the Tower, which was both, a palace and a prison.
4. Heathrow, which is one of the most impressive airports in the world, is one of London's two big airports.
5. People often visit the Thames Flood Barrier, which protects London against floods.

Seite 43 Lösungen zu Übung 16

1. who
2. which
3. who
4. which
5. which
6. which
7. which
8. which, which
9. who, which

Seite 45 Lösungen zu Übung 17

1. Aunt Barbara, who has bought a new car, will visit us next week.
2. This is the book which you were looking for.
3. The girl who wears a red dress really gets on my nerves.
4. Sue believes in the existence of the Loch Ness monster, which she has never seen. Sue who believes in the existence of the Loch Ness monster has never seen it.
5. Andrew can't remember the name of the boy who has red hair.

Seite 46 Lösungen zu Übung 18

1. who
2. that / which
3. that / which
4. that / which
5. who, who
6. who
7. that / which
8. who, that / who
9. who
10. which
11. that / who

Seite 48 Lösungen zu Übung 19

1. that
2. that / which
3. that
4. that / which
5. that
6. that

Lösungen zu Übung 20

Seite 49

1. You certainly remember Joe whose mother writes detective stories.
2. Alan whose father works for the White House is the boy down there.
3. I haven't found Mary-Ann yet whose grandmother never goes out.
4. I know you want to meet Jim whose brother is very good at skating.
5. Do you remember Doreen whose guinea pig loves eating candy?

Lösungen zu Übung 21

Seite 50

1. who
2. whose
3. who
4. who
5. whose
6. who
7. whose
8. who, who
9. whose
10. who, whose

Passiv

Lösungen zu Übung 22

Seite 55

1. had been taken
2. had been done
3. were invited
4. was planned
5. are brought along
6. are baked, are cooked, are bought
7. can't (cannot/can not) be drunk
8. will be taken out

Lösungen zu Übung 23

Seite 56

1. She was seen at 8 o'clock in the morning.
2. Hundreds of new stamps have been bought.
3. The desk will be moved closer to the window.
4. The job will have been done by noon.
5. Many mistakes are made today.
6. Flowers are sold every day.
7. The border may not be passed.

Lösungen zu Übung 24

Seite 57

1. General Custer's troops were attacked on June 25th, 1876 by Sioux Indians.
2. All of Custer's men were killed.
3. The incident was called 'The Battle of the Little Bighorn'.
4. The Indians were regarded as devils by white Americans.
5. Much later, a monument was built on the battlefield by the American government.
6. Every year, the monument is visited by thousands of tourists.
7. The Indians aren't (are not) seen as devils any more.

Radiere falsche Lösungen aus. Bearbeite diese Aufgaben noch einmal.

1. Wiederholung Lösungen zu W 1.1

Seite 60

1. went on **a** trip
2. 200 miles **a** day
3. rented **an** expensive car
4. went to Chicago, met **a** friend of my dad's
5. is **a** dentist
6. was **a** soldier, once **a** year
7. three relatives **a** week, to keep in contact
8. has **a** friend
9. is **a** policewoman
10. is **a** Muslim
11. once **a** year
12. such nice people
    ('people' = «Leute» ist Plural, deshalb ist 'a' hier nicht möglich)
13. as **a** girl
14. loved **a** Christian feast
15. Once **a** girl-friend, her for Christmas
16. what an exciting event
17. quite **a** lot, to know real Americans, for **a** long time

Seite 62 Lösungen zu W 1.2

1. One day, Professor Know-All was thinking of a wonderful new machine, when Mr Smart came to visit him.
2. Professor Know-All asked his guest to sit down. Soon they were having tea. ('Have tea' ist nicht statisch.)
3. Mr Smart asked his host, "What have you been working on?"
4. Professor Know-All had been thinking about a new toy for children.
5. But he wasn't (was not) going to tell Mr Smart about it.
6. Professor Know-All thought, "Tomorrow I will be developing a new automatic bird that can fly and sing."
7. In the middle of my work, Little Georgie will come over and ask me for a toy. He won't (will not) be sitting still in my lab.
8. He will be jumping around even more when I will give him the new toy that I am going to call 'Hootchy-kootchy'.

Seite 63 Lösungen zu W 1.3

1. who
2. who
3. whose, that/who
4. whose
5. that
6. that/who
7. that
8. that
9. that/who

Lösungen zu W 1.4

Seite 64

1. The 'West Side Story' was done by the Musical Company.
2. Breakfast had been eaten.
3. The dialogue was being read.
4. The short story was read by Jimmy.
5. The unit will have been repeated before the testing day.
6. Several shooting stars have been seen by Karen and Billy.
7. The London marathon is being run by Werner.
8. A good job has been done on this exercise.

2. Wiederholung

Lösungen zu W 2.1

Seite 66

1. Uncle John is a musician.
2. He often goes to concerts but he loves all concerts that are given in churches.
3. The church he likes most is St. Anna's Church.
4. He thinks the acoustics are best there.
5. Uncle John plays the piano and the cello.
6. He plays the piano with his friend Roberto who is a doctor and he plays the flute with his friend Pierre who is a hairdresser.
7. Roberto is an Italian and Pierre is a Frenchman.
8. Roberto is quite a good friend of Uncle John's.
9. Twice a week they meet and play together.
10. Most of the time they play Mozart.
11. Uncle John says that most musicians love Mozart.
12. He is rather an expert on Mozart.
13. He says that life is more interesting if you love music.
14. Art makes you always happy.

Lösungen zu W 2.2

Seite 67

1. lived
2. was travelling, got
3. don't (do not) make
4. was cutting, left
5. wrote, are abusing / abuse
6. is, was
7. did not write
8. were photographing

Radiere falsche Lösungen aus. Bearbeite diese Aufgaben noch einmal.

Seite 68 Lösungen zu W 2.3

1. who
2. that/who
3. which
4. that
5. that
6. that/which
7. which
8. that/who
9. whose

Seite 69 Lösungen zu W 2.4

1. Pupils' drawings are being looked at by the art teacher.
2. Seven photographers were arrested by the police.
3. Three more of them could have been arrested.
4. Flies and other small insects are eaten by spiders.
5. Yesterday the London Symphony Orchestra was conducted by Sir Yehudi Menuhin.
6. Dublin will be visited by Grade 13.
7. London had been seen before.

So gut warst du: Die Lösungen und Bewertungen der Tests

Lösungen zu Test 1: Der Artikel

Seite 71

1. is **a** Catholic
2. was **a** Protestant, goes to church
3. at **the** church, is in hospital
4. go to **the** hospital, should give him flowers
5. remember **the** whiskey, travelled 50 miles **a** day, 40 miles in half **a** day
6. was **a** paper boy, 15 days vacation **a** year, As **a** paper boy, £ 4 **a** week
7. As **a** youngster, What **a** good time, quite **a** good friend

Lösungen zu Test 2: Die 'progressive form'

Seite 73

1. Mr Smart said, "I'm (I am) sitting here, and I'm (I am) talking to you."	**4 Punkte**
2. I should be calling my business partner and tell him what I bought."	**2 Punkte**
3. Professor Know-All was astonished and asked, "Are you going to produce thousands of 'Hootchy-kootchies'?	**3 Punkte**
4. I thought that you bought the toy for your son. What was I dreaming of?"	**3 Punkte**
5. Mr Smart was smiling when he heard that.	**2 Punkte**
6. Professor Know-All understood that he had not been paying attention. He had signed a paper. It must have been a contract.	**3 Punkte**
7. When the professor was throwing him out, Mr Smart said, "It has been nice to do business with you, Professor."	**2 Punkte**

Lösungen zu Test 3: Die Relativpronomen

Seite 75

1. who, which	7. whose
2. that	8. who, who
3. that/which	9. who
4. which	10. which
5. that	11. whose, that
6. who	12. that/which

Lösungen zu Test 4: Das Passiv

Seite 77

1. a) The winner was given a gold medal.	*(2 Punkte für die richtige Verbform*	**a) 3 Punkte**
b) A gold medal was given to the winner.	*nur einmal in a/b.)*	**b) 1 Punkt**
2. Tomorrow's discussions will be led by the chairperson.		**4 Punkte**
3. All air traffic was stopped by storm and heavy rain.		**4 Punkte**
4. A lot of applause was being given.		**3 Punkte**
5. All the neighbours would have been informed.		**3 Punkte**
6. The school has not been informed about the child's absence by Thomas' parents.		**4 Punkte**

Immer dabei: Das Lesezeichen

Schneide das letzte Blatt aus und falte es entlang der schwarzen Linie. (Schlau ist es, wenn du dir die Seite 95 vorher kopierst – falls du das Lesezeichen einmal verlegen solltest.) Jetzt hast du ein tolles Lesezeichen, auf dem du immer schnell nachschauen kannst, wenn dir die Bedeutungen bestimmter Fachbegriffe nicht mehr einfallen. (Wenn du Lust hast, kannst du das Lesezeichen unten lochen und dort einen dicken Wollfaden oder Ähnliches durchziehen. Dann ist es noch auffälliger.)

Artikel (article)

Vor Vokalanlaut:
Bestimmter Artikel
(definite article) – the [ðiː]
Unbestimmter Artikel
(indefinite article) – an [æn]

Vor Konsonantenanlaut:
Bestimmter Artikel
(definite article) – the [ðə]
Unbestimmter Artikel
(indefinite article) – a [ə]

Relativpronomen (relative pronoun)

Relativpronomen beziehen sich auf vorher genannte Nomen.
Die Relativpronomen 'who' oder 'that' verweisen
- auf **Personen** und **Haustiere mit Eigennamen**.

Die Relativpronomen 'which' oder 'that' verweisen
- auf **andere Tiere**, auf **Sachen** und **Abstrakta.**

Für alle Relativpronomen lautet der **Genitiv 'whose'.**

Zeichensetzung bei Relativsätzen

Zwischen Hauptsatz und **notwendigem** Relativsatz steht **kein** Komma.
Zwischen Hauptsatz und **nicht notwendigem** Relativsatz **steht ein Komma.**

'progressive form' (Verlaufsform)

Bildung: Form von 'be' + Vollverb + 'ing' (*present participle* des Vollverbs).
Die 'progressive form' wird in eine bestimmte Zeit gesetzt, indem 'be' in diese Zeit gesetzt wird.

Passiv (passive voice)

Verbform
Form von 'be' + 3. Form
(past participle) des Vollverbs

Passivsatz
Hat der Aktivsatz *(active voice sentence)* nur ein direktes Objekt *(direct object)*, wird dies zum Subjekt des Passivsatzes.

Hat der Aktivsatz ein direktes und ein indirektes Objekt *(indirect object)*, kann jedes von beiden zum Subjekt des Passivsatzes werden. Das indirekte Objekt wird jedoch als neues Subjekt bevorzugt.

Das Subjekt des Aktivsatzes wird nur dann zum *by-agent* des Passivsatzes, wenn es wichtig und aussagekräftig ist.

3609/3